On Loan

"We got to do something quick, Sylvie," I told her as I tried to huddle into my coat.

"Lyon's right. Can't you see he's right?" Justin pleaded.

Sylvie took a deep breath, looked down at the baby, and lifted the blanket away from its face. Then she looked up at me and in a choking voice said, "All right, we'll give the baby to Miss Adeline Newberry — on a loan."

There was no time to argue about that.

"How are we going to do it, Lyon?" Justin asked me. "We can't just knock on the door and shove it into her arms."

"We'll have to put the baby in front of her door and knock and run," I said, feeling afraid just thinking about it. I sure was talking braver than I felt.

**Other Apple Paperbacks
you will enjoy:**

Aliens in the Family
by Margaret Mahy

With You and Without You
by Ann M. Martin

Last One Home
by Mary Pope Osborne

Hurricane Elaine
by Johanna Hurwitz

Mystery of the Witches' Bridge
by Barbee Oliver Carlton

Baby-Snatcher
by Susan Terris

MIRACLE at CLEMENT'S POND

Patricia Pendergraft

AN
APPLE
PAPERBACK

SCHOLASTIC INC.
New York Toronto London Auckland Sydney

ISBN 0-590-41458-5

12 11 10 9 8 7 6 5 4 3   2 3/9

Printed in the U.S.A.   01

First Scholastic printing, April 1988

*This book is dedicated
with love to Lisa Marie.*

Contents

1
We Find More Than Bullfrogs at Clement's Pond

Well, if you want to know the truth, and I guess you do, I mean, what would be the point of lying about it now? You'd be sure to run into someone in Clement's Pond who knows the whole story and find out I'd lied, so I'm going to tell the whole truth and nothing but, just like my Aunt Ester said I should. She said if I told the truth, I'd get some mighty big blessings in life, but if I didn't tell the truth, the way she said it was, for sure and for certain, I'd get a plague of damnation on me. So this is the way it all happened — cross my heart and stick a thousand needles in my eyes, if it ain't.

When we put the baby on Adeline Newberry's front porch, we thought it would make her joyful and happy, just like the way she was always telling everyone in Clement's Pond she'd be if she had a little baby to take care of. Being the only old maid in Clement's Pond was a pretty hard cross to bear. She was childless and all alone and all she had to love was the chickens that pecked around in the dust in her yard and a stray dog or two whenever one wandered onto her property. She had been jilted by Ferdie Hughs when she was young and no one else in town ever looked at her twice. Leastways, not with marriage on their minds. Except maybe old man Oscar Bebee, who flirts with all the women in church and out, and he ain't exactly a good catch for any woman. He lumbers around town on a cane and spits tobaccer juice all over wherever he happens to be. Aunt Ester said it ain't likely any woman, even Adeline Newberry, would want to spend the rest of her life washing tobaccer stains off her shoes.

I couldn't rightly put my finger on why no one wanted Adeline Newberry. It wasn't that Adeline was ugly. There are lots of old ladies in Clement's Pond uglier and fatter and even skinnier than Adeline. And it wasn't that she had a physical deformity neither, like the hunchback Gypsy who lives in the woods and only comes out once in a blue moon and, when she does, goes up and down the road looking for lost change.

"Maybe it's because Adeline has false teeth," Sylvie Bogart said once. Sylvie is Justin Bogart's sister, and Justin is my best friend in all the world.

"That's stupid," I told Sylvie. "My Aunt Ester has got false teeth. I seen them in a cup of water lots of times. That didn't keep her from getting married to Uncle Clayborn."

"Maybe she didn't have them false teeth when

your Uncle Clayborn married her," Sylvie said sarcastically.

But it wasn't the teeth and it wasn't the way Adeline looked. She had a right fine cushion of fat on her and plenty of what Aunt Ester called "get up and go." Her eyes was dark and kind, and according to Aunt Ester, any gent in his right mind ought to be glad to get a good woman like Adeline Newberry. But they weren't and it just seemed Adeline was the loneliest person in all of Clement's Pond. Just about every time she come to visit Aunt Ester, she'd start in telling how lonely she was.

"If I had me a little baby . . ." she'd start out, until Aunt Ester would cut right in and tell her, "You're too old for a baby, Adeline Newberry!"

"But, if I had one . . ."

"You won't have one!" Aunt Ester would tell her flatly.

"But, if I did . . ."

"All right, what would you do with a baby *if* you had one?" Aunt Ester would stare over the top of her glasses at Adeline with eyes so sharp they could bore a hole through a plank of wood.

But Adeline didn't pay no attention to that. She'd get a look on her face and fix a stare on some far-off place and say, "Oh, I'd hold it and love it and take grand care of it. I'd dress it up every day just like as if I was taking it to church and I'd make it cute little clothes and order some, too, out of the Sears and Roebuck catalog. And I'd curl its hair and teach it all kinds of fine manners. I'd never let it cry or be afraid . . ."

"You'd spoil it rotten!" Aunt Ester would snort with a loud smack of her lips.

"Yes, Ester, I would. I'd spoil it like a little baby ought to be spoiled. With all the love and tenderness I got inside me," Adeline would say, pulling her eyes back from the far-off place and fixing them on Aunt Ester.

"Well, you may as well get them notions out of your head, Adeline. You ain't married and you're too old to have a baby even if you was," Aunt Ester would tell her like she was an authority on the subject.

A brave, sunny look would appear on Adeline's face; then suddenly a curtain, like the heavy fog that hangs over the pond in winter, would take its place. She'd sigh and look down at her ringless wedding-band finger and say in a low voice, "Well, I reckon you're right, Ester."

So I reckon you can see why we wanted to make Adeline Newberry happy. But the way we got the baby was, Sylvie and Justin and me went down to the pond one evening late to go froggin'. There was a chill coming up in the wind by the time we got halfway there but we just kept trudging along, hoping to lose Sylvie along the way. Seemed like there was times when we just couldn't shake her off us. Just as we got near enough to see the water in the pond, we heard a strange sniffling noise like a girl was crying and a man's voice saying in a short, gruff way, "Aw, come on, Fleur. It won't do no good to cry. You know someone will come along. Any minute, too. This place is thick with all kinds of people, day and night."

That just seemed to make the girl cry harder and the man said in an angry, impatient voice, "You hadn't got no money to take care of it no way! Come on now!"

The girl sniffled again and said something real quiet and soft that we couldn't understand and, right after that, we heard a rustle in the underbrush and the movement of the tree limbs that hang low over the pond, and soon after that, the sound of a car door slamming shut and someone driving away in it real fast. We could hear the pebbles and dirt kick up under the wheels of the car as it spun away.

"What do you suppose they left over there?" Justin asked.

"Maybe they robbed a bank over to Tylersville and are hiding the money until they can come back for it. Maybe J. Edgar Hoover is on their trail —"

"Aw, shoot," Justin snorted, cutting Sylvie off just as she got going good. "You listen to the radio too much."

"J. Edgar Hoover is the busiest man in the whole world!" I spoke up. "Ain't he the head of the FBI? He wouldn't go after plain old robbers. Besides, you heard what the man said, Sylvie. He said they ain't got no money to take care of whatever it is."

"Maybe it's a hurt puppy," Sylvie said. "Or a cat in a gunnysack. Folks is always dropping kittens off around here."

"Aw, shoot!" Justin snorted disgustedly.

Me and Sylvie follered Justin to where the sniffling and talking come from and pushed the low branches and vines out of our way. Up in the darkness of one of the trees a whippoorwill set up a fuss.

"Holy pinchin' earwigs!" Justin shouted, looking down.

Me and Sylvie leaned close and looked down too. "A baby!" Sylvie cried. "It's a baby!"

"Why would anyone leave a baby here?" Justin asked, frowning hard.

"I don't know, but I know one thing — it will die, sure as a frog has legs, if we leave it here," I said, staring hard at that little baby. It was sound asleep. We could see its little face in the moonlight that was slowly creeping up over the pond. It was wrapped up in a heavy blanket like as if the person who left it there wanted it to stay nice and warm.

"I guess we ought to take it to the police station — " Justin started, and Sylvie cut him off quick.

"No!" she cried. "The police will only put it in a place with some old mangy folks who might not even want it," Sylvie rushed on.

"How do you know what the police'll do?" I asked her.

"I heard tell. And sometimes them mangy folks lock the babies up in a room and tie them to a bed and let them starve."

"We could take the baby to your Aunt Ester, Lyon," Justin said.

"We can't do that! Aunt Ester would take it to the police for sure."

"Well, maybe we should just leave it here," Justin said, staring down at the baby again.

"There's bound to be people around here to-morrow."

"Justin Bogart! How can you even think about leaving this little baby here all night long?" Sylvie cried. "It might rain so hard the water would rise and this baby would float right into it and get drowned."

"And what if old man Lyman's half-starved red hound come along?" I said. "Or Oscar Bebee's bull got out of the pasture or a snake come crawling up . . ." I shuddered, just thinking about all the things that could happen to that baby. And I guess I sounded like Sylvie, because Justin give me a disgusted look.

"Well, what are we going to do?" Justin asked impatiently.

Sylvie squatted down and her hand moved gently over the blanket to make sure it covered the baby good and snug.

"I want to keep it, that's what I want to do. I want to keep it and play with it," Sylvie said softly.

Justin laughed, then snorted and threw his head up to the sky and laughed again. "Listen to her! She thinks it's an old doll!"

"You shut up, Justin! I'm a mind to take this baby home and put it in my playhouse in the backyard that Daddy built for me and play with it every day."

"What would you do when Mama and Daddy found out?" Justin asked, still laughing.

"I'd . . . well, I'd say . . . I'd say it was Taffy's little cousin from over to Tylersville or something."

"Taffy don't have no cousin. Taffy don't even have a sister ner brother. All Taffy's got is her mean old mama and a big wall-eyed cat her mama kicks the wind out of nine times a day and twice on Sunday," Justin snarled.

"You be quiet about Taffy! Taffy Marshall is my best friend!"

"You got to feed a baby, Sylvie," I told her. "You got to have milk and mashed pertaters and gravy too."

"And you know Mama ain't going to buy no extry milk ner nothing else for no baby," Justin said.

Sylvie picked the baby up gently and gathered it close into her arms and we all stared down into its little face. "Ain't no way I'm going to leave this baby here," she said like she was filled with fire. The baby didn't make a move or a sound, and just about then the wind started chattering in the trees and little sprinkles of rain started dripping down through the branches. We stood a little closer and watched its face.

"I ain't never been this close to a baby before," I said.

"Me neither," Justin said.

"Well, they're just persons," Sylvie told us softly. "They're just little persons and there ain't no reason to be afraid of them."

The wind started whipping at the baby's blanket and we watched its little nose twitch like it was getting ready to wake up. Sylvie held it a little closer, and we started walking, with me and Justin pushing the low branches and tangled vines out of the way so Sylvie could carry the baby without stumbling or having a twig hit the baby.

"We better head for the police station," Justin said, pulling his collar up close to his neck.

"Maybe Justin is right," I said, and Sylvie turned eyes of fury on me.

"Whose side are you on, Lyon Savage? I thought you was my boyfriend! I thought you was my true love that would do anything I asked of you, that would be on my side, no matter what. I thought — "

"I *am* your boyfriend, Sylvie. I *am* your true love," I told her dismally. "But I don't know about doing just anything you ask of me."

Sylvie stopped walking and her eyes went through me like the prongs on a pitchfork. "Didn't we prick our palms with your Aunt Ester's sewing needle and didn't we hold hands and let our blood run together and make a true-love vow?"

I thought I'd get a headache for sure, just thinking about that time. It was all Sylvie's idea. She said if the blood of two people run together, that meant they was true loves forever and ever. Even after I did it, I wondered how much "ever and ever" I wanted of Sylvie.

Me and Justin stopped walking and I looked straight into Sylvie's eyes that sometimes looked so transparent, it seemed I could look right through them to her soul. "We did that. But we didn't vow nothing about no baby," I told her.

"A true-love vow takes in all dimensions of life," Sylvie stated with a toss of her head.

There was a quick, bright flash and we looked up. Smoky-colored clouds was racing across the sky, blotting out the moon. It was an eerie look. Just like the end of the world might come. And, all at once, through the pine trees, we heard the rumble of thunder. We started running, heading away from the pond as fast as we could go. Sylvie carried the baby hugged up close to her, careful to see that its head was covered by the blanket and protected from the wind and rain. The rain started coming down harder, making a loud tap-tap noise as it hit the tangles of vines and branches along the road that led away from the pond.

"Where are we going?" Justin asked as we ran.

"Uncle Jack Spicer's house is just around the corner where that clump of tall elm trees is. We'd better stop there," I panted.

"Uncle Jack's house don't even protect all them fleas he's got in it!" Justin said through heavy breaths. "It's got so many holes in the roof that the rain floods the place every winter!"

"We can sit on the porch," I said. "Uncle Jack will never know."

Sylvie slowed down and looked up into the sky. "I guess we'd better stop there. It's liable to come a flood that'll drowned every old bullfrog around the pond. We can't let Uncle Jack know about the baby, though. No matter what happens!"

2
Miss Adeline
Gets Her Wish

Uncle Jack Spicer lived all alone in an old rattle-trap house that was falling apart at every joint. He was always fixing and fiddling on it, but he never got much done to improve it. Everyone figured it took him about sixteen years just to put a new roof on, and by the time he'd finished that, it sprung about two hundred more leaks and he had to start all over patching and hammering on it again. There was all kinds of junk and clutter all over the yard, including three old junk cars in the backyard with weeds all growed up around them and a big use-to-be sailing boat that had a hole in the hull. He was always going to take it out someday and sail off to a place he called "Shangri-La," where he said all his dreams would come true. Inside the house was no better. Six cats lived in there with Uncle Jack and wandered in and out whenever a door was left open. Uncle Jack fed them off the floor and it wasn't nothing to walk into his kitchen and slip on cat food or in a puddle of milk. In a front winder of the house was a sign that said:

NEVER MIND THE BULLDOG
BEWARE OF THE OWNER

No one worried about Uncle Jack, though. Unless it was a stranger passing by who saw the sign and kept going. Uncle Jack was kind to everyone. He wasn't really no one's uncle. Folks just called him that.

We went up the sagging, creaking front steps of the porch real quiet. Sylvie sat down in front of the winder on the old tattered divan that had about a zillion cat hairs in it and hunched the baby up real close in her arms, while Justin and me stood around listening for Uncle Jack and the cats. The rain sounded like bricks tossed against the tin roof of the porch. It was as loud as thunder when it rumbles across Clement's Pond.

"When this baby wakes up, it's going to be hungry," Sylvie whispered. "It will want milk. Warm milk."

"Uncle Jack ought to have some," I said, remembering all them cats and how they was always lapping up milk from old cracked bowls Uncle Jack left on the floor for them.

"You reckon we ought to wake him up?" Justin asked.

"No! We can't do that!" Sylvie gasped. "We'd have to tell him about the baby if we did that!"

"Sylvie, we are going to have to tell someone. It wouldn't be fair or right for you to keep that little baby," I said, keeping my voice low.

"And you can believe that!" Justin added with a snort.

Sylvie sighed and pursed her lips all up and looked down grimly at the baby.

"Who's out there? Who's on my porch?" Uncle Jack's voice roared out of the house and made us all three leap toward the porch steps.

We was down them steps in nothing flat. "Who's out there, I said," Uncle Jack roared again and I could imagine him running through the house hitching up the suspenders on his pants and yanking his shotgun down from the wall.

We beat a path across the yard and bolted out onto the mushy, rain-soaked road just as a light flashed on in Uncle Jack's house. Sylvie, even though she was carrying the baby, was a faster runner than me and Justin. She had already made it to Adeline Newberry's front gate and was looking back, waiting for us to catch up. When we reached her, she was panting and clutching the baby so tightly it looked like she was going to squeeze it to death.

"It's waking up!" she whispered, all out of breath. "What are we going to do? What if it starts crying?"

We saw a circle of light flash out onto the road, coming from Uncle Jack's yard.

"It's a lantern!" Justin hissed.

We watched and waited, shuddering with fear, but the light went away. I guess Uncle Jack didn't want to go out into the rain looking for no one.

We was shivering and so tired and out of breath we could hardly stand or think. No part of me was dry. The baby started wiggling in Sylvie's arms and made a small whimpering sound. Sylvie rocked it gently against her shoulder and whispered, "Hush, little baby. You hush up now . . . hush . . . hush . . ."

Lightning struck somewhere close by and lit up the whole sky and thunder come right on its heels, crashing so loud it seemed to vibrate the ground under our feet. The baby let out a cry and we run through the gate and huddled together beneath the chestnut tree in Adeline Newberry's yard.

"Oh, hush, baby . . . hush, please hush," Sylvie said desperately as she rocked the baby back and forth in her arms. But the baby only cried louder and the blanket moved where its little feet was.

"That's a hungry cry, if I ever heard one," Justin said with his teeth chattering.

"We've got to *do* something." Sylvie's eyes was on me, like she thought I'd have the answer of what to do. But all I could think about was how warm and cozy Adeline Newberry's little house looked right smack in front of us, and how clean and dry her front porch looked.

Adeline Newberry's place wasn't anything like Uncle Jack Spicer's. Her yard was clean and filled with flowers and trees, and she never dropped a tool anywhere that I knew of and just left it. Her house always smelled like sweet, fragrant talcum powder and fresh-cut flowers and whatever she happened to be cooking on the stove. Like as not she'd have a soup bone boiling in a pot or a cake in the oven, and the smell would be all over the house and yard. Many's the time my nose follered the delicious smell of baked cookies right up to her front door. Adeline was always good for a handout of cookies and lemonade, and she wouldn't let no kid go away hungry that come to her door. And . . . as I stared at her cozy little house, I was counting on that.

"Sylvie," I said, and I had to stop and clear my throat. She just stared at me out of them blue eyes and hung on to that baby. "Sylvie, I can tell you've taken a right smart liking to this here little baby, but it don't seem right for you to keep it when there is others in this world who could use a baby more than you . . ."

"What do you mean, Lyon?" Sylvie asked with her eyes narrowed at me.

"Well" — I had an itch in my throat that even clearing wouldn't scratch — "well, you got so much schoolwork to do and helping your mama around the house and such . . ." Suddenly Sylvie hugged that baby up so close to her, I thought for sure she'd squeeze it in two. It was plain she already loved it with a strong passion.

"Lyon's right, Sylvie," Justin spoke up like he was pleading. "You'd be so busy all the time, you couldn't do no sneakin' and hidin'. You wouldn't be able to take proper care of that baby at all."

"What . . . what are we g-going to d-do?"

Sylvie asked, and I knew it wasn't just the rain on her cheeks. There was tears mixed in there too.

"Sylvie," I said as gently as I could, "who do you know in Clement's Pond who has just about disgusted everyone with her eternal jabbering about babies and how she'd give anything to have one? Who do you know who could really give a little baby like this one here in your arms a real good home and lots of special attention and love? Who . . . ?"

I didn't have to say another word. Sylvie turned and looked at Adeline Newberry's house. "Adeline," she whispered, and her voice was almost lost in the wind and the rain and the sound of the thunder soaring over the valley.

"There ain't no one who wants a baby more," I said as kind as I could.

"Old Adeline would sure love to have that baby," Justin said.

Sylvie turned back and looked at me. Her eyes was huge and filled with tears and rain. "This is *my* baby," she said fiercely.

"It ain't yours!" Justin exploded as the rain slipped and slid all over his face.

Sylvie tightened her arms around the baby and glared at me and Justin. "It's *mine*, I told you! And I aim to keep it! I'll get Taffy to help me take care of it."

"Taffy can't help you!" Justin practically yelled; then he brought his voice down real low. "Her mama would wallop her from here to Tylersville and back again if she was to find out about you having this baby!"

"She wouldn't have to know," Sylvie said uncertainly.

"She'd find out, though. Then where would you be?"

Sylvie looked down at the baby. "I don't know," she said, and she could barely talk.

"We got to give it to Adeline, Sylvie. It's . . . well, like the Lord hisself led us right here to her house, right here to the very woman who wants a baby more than anyone in the whole world." I was trembling all over. It looked like there was no way to get that baby away from Sylvie.

"It's a fact that Adeline wants a baby, all right." Sylvie's words slid off into the air just like the raindrops sliding off the leaves of the chestnut tree we was standing under.

"She wants a baby even more than you, Sylvie," I said, trying to gentle my voice.

All at once the sky lit up with streaks of lightning that looked like Fourth of July firecrackers. Then before a feller could start counting backwards, thunder boomed in our ears like someone beating on Aunt Ester's washtub with a hammer. It started raining even harder.

"We got to do something quick, Sylvie," I told her as I tried to huddle up into my coat.

"Lyon's right. Can't you see he's right?" Justin pleaded.

Sylvie took a deep breath, looked down at the baby, and lifted the blanket away from its face. Seemed like she just stared at it for a mighty long time before she bent her head and kissed it. Then she looked up at me and in a choking voice said, "All right, I'll give my baby to Miss Adeline Newberry — on a loan."

There was no time to argue about that.

"How are we going to do it, Lyon?" Justin asked me. "We can't just knock on the door and shove it into her arms."

"We'll have to put the baby in front of her door and knock and run," I said, feeling afraid just thinking about it. But I knew it was the only way to give Adeline that baby without her knowing about me and Sylvie and Justin.

"What if she don't come to the door?" Justin asked.

"We'll stay right here and watch and make sure she does," I told him. I sure was talking braver than I felt.

We started walking across the wet, gushy yard and crept up the steps of Adeline's porch as silently as one of Uncle Jack's old tomcats. The porch was nice and dry and the place where Sylvie laid the baby was as clean as the inside of Adeline's whole house.

"So long, but not good-bye," Sylvie whispered to the baby as she leaned down and kissed it. And when she walked away, she turned and kissed the tips of her fingers and blew the kiss away to the baby.

Justin and I give a good knock and run, but no one come. Then, as we stood huddled under the chestnut tree, the baby started crying again. It sounded so forlorn and sad that Sylvie threatened to go back up on the porch and get it.

"That baby is crying because I put it down! Because it already learned to love me!" Sylvie cried. "I'm leaving it here now, but I'm not giving it up!"

The tone of Sylvie's voice made her words sound so much like a threat that it made me swaller and stare hard at her, but just as I opened my mouth to give her a comeback, the whole house exploded with light. Every winder lit up and the front door sprang open and Adeline Newberry poked her head out. We all moved closer together in the dripping shadows of the chestnut tree and sucked in our breath.

Long brownish-gray braids fell across Adeline's shoulders like the knotted ropes in Uncle Clayborn's barn, as she pulled her white gown up close around her and peered out onto the porch. It only took a blink of an eye for her to look down and discover where the crying was coming from.

"Why, the Lord have mercy . . ." she cried like she couldn't believe her eyes, and she bent down and lifted the baby up in her arms and stared at it. "Where in the world did you come from?" she asked, looking into the baby's face. She looked so astonished, she didn't even look like herself.

After a minute or two she walked to the edge of the porch and looked up and down the road like she thought she might see who had left the baby, but it was raining so hard, she couldn't of seen anyone on the road if they'd been there.

We kept holding our breath and crossing our fingers and praying that Adeline wouldn't see us under the chestnut tree as her eyes skirted the yard. Then, another crack of thunder and flash of lightning shot over the sky, and Adeline whipped around and hurried back across the porch and into the house. The door shut just as another flash of lightning exploded. In that split second, I looked into Sylvie's face. Her lips and chin was trembling and rainy tears was washing all down her face.

"We'd better go now," I said.

"Maybe we should wait until Adeline turns off the lights," Justin said nervously.

"She'll be up all night with that baby," Sylvie said with a loud sniffle. "She'll be feeding it and getting it warmed up and trying to figure out how it got on the porch and . . ." She stopped and took a deep breath and sniffled again.

"Come on," I said, and we dashed for the gate and snuck out it as quickly as we'd snuck through it, and run down the road with our shoes sinking into the gushy mud. We reached my house first because it was closest to Adeline's house.

"We've all got to promise we won't tell a word about the baby to no one," I said when we stopped running.

"Why, Lyon, that goes without saying," Sylvie said.

"We'd better all promise, just the same."

"I sure do promise," Justin said.

"Me too," I said.

Me and Justin looked at Sylvie and waited.

"You don't have to caution me about it, Lyon," she said.

"Promise!" Justin demanded.

"All right, I promise," Sylvie said, but it sounded mighty grudging to me.

We parted then and I turned and run through the muddy path that led to the house and banged on the front door. By the time Aunt Ester got to the door and let me in, Sylvie and Justin had disappeared into the rain.

3
I Hear
My Favorite Story Again

"Iffen you been out froggin' in this weather, I've been out calling hogs!" Aunt Ester blasted in my face as soon as I walked through the door. "Just look at you! Soaked to the very core and dripping like a rain cloud! Where have you been, boy?"

I swallered painfully, pushed my sopping hair up out of my face, and started to tremble. A big puddle of rainwater was dripping off my clothes and forming in a circle on the floor around my feet.

"Well, never mind that now," Aunt Ester said sharply. "Go get out of them wet clothes and wrap yourself up in that big Choctaw Indian blanket Bear brought the last time he come. I'll turn on the oven in the kitchen range and you can sit in front of it until you get thawed out good."

I did what Aunt Ester told me to do. I went into my room, pulled off my soaked clothes, threw them across the bedstead, and got the Choctaw Indian blanket that Bear brought and wrapped myself all up in it. Then I went back into the kitchen and set down in the hard-backed chair Aunt Ester had pulled out for me in front of the open oven door. Behind me I could hear Aunt Ester stirring up a cup of hot tea for me. I looked down into the little hole in the stove where I could see the fire spitting red and blue and yeller, and I thought about Bear.

"Like the feller says, this weather ain't fit for man ner beast," Aunt Ester said behind me. "And iffen it ain't fit for man ner beast, it most sure ain't fit for a boy!"

"Aunt Ester?"

"Yes, boy?"

"When is Bear coming back?"

I could hear the spoon Aunt Ester held tinking against the inside of the cup as she stirred it round and round in the hot tea. The flame in the little hole licked and lapped and made a hissing noise. I huddled deeper into the scratchy warm Choctaw Indian blanket.

"He'll be a-coming back. Bear will be a-coming back in the spring. You can be sure of that, boy," Aunt Ester said, and I could feel her eyes on the back of me.

"Tell me the story again, Aunt Ester. Tell me the story about me and Bear and — "

"Oh my, boy. You want that story again? Why, I just told it to you the other night. Don't you never get enough of it?"

Seemed like, because of finding the baby and all, I wanted to hear the story worse than I ever did before. "I like to hear it, Aunt Ester," I said, and when I looked up, Aunt Ester was standing beside me, smiling down at me.

"Of course you do," she said gently, and her hand reached down and rubbed the back of my head. "Of course you do." She handed me the cup and pulled up her own favorite sunk-in-the-seat chair, set down beside me, took in a deep breath, and stared down into the flame inside the little hole in the stove along with me.

"Well," she said, and she took in another deep breath that brought her shoulders up, then down, and she began. "Well, Lyon Savage, when your daddy, when Bear, heard you was born, he come flying back here to Clement's Pond all the way from Canada like he had sprouted wings and could fly all by hisself. Him being such a free spirit, folks never would of dreamed just how proud he was. Why, he was the proudest father in a hundred miles around, to have a son. Of course, your mama passing on like she done when you was born was a pain in his big old heart that nearly took all the spirit plumb out of him. But when he saw you, his own little son, the spirit come rushing back into him. You was laying on your mama's granny-square quilt, nekkid as a little jaybird, and the first thing Bear said was how he'd seen little lion cubs that twisted and tried to move around just like you did. He sort of laughed the way he does and said, 'Ester, I'm going to call my boy Lyon.' And Zooie Marshall, when she heard, said, 'How come you'd give a baby a name like that, Bear?

Lyon . . . Lyon . . .' She said the name over and then she said, 'That's a mean name, Bear!' And Bear laughed his laugh and told her, 'No meaner than Bear Savage!' "

I looked up at Aunt Ester. Tears was sparkling in her gray, sleepy eyes and the heat from the oven had turned her wrinkles pink and soft-looking.

"Aunt Ester?"

"Yes, honey?" She wiped her eyes with the back of her hand and looked at me.

"I wish Bear didn't go away so much."

"I wish it too, Lyon. But, just as you can't harness the wind ner tell the sun when to rise and set, you can't tell Bear Savage what to do."

"I wish I could, though," I said softly, looking back down into the little flame. "I sure do wish I could."

"Hush now, boy, and drink your tea while it's good and hot. It'll warm your insides and ward off a cold," Aunt Ester said; then she added sternly, "The next time you stay out in weather like this, you'll find more than a cup of tea waiting for you!"

I snuggled deeper into the Choctaw Indian blanket and stared up at the jars of blueberry preserves on the shelf in a corner. Then I took a sip of tea. It was so hot and tasted so awful, I wanted to spit it up as it burned down my throat. We were quiet; then after a while I said, "Aunt Ester?"

"Yes, boy?"

"Did you ever hear the name Fleur?"

"Fleur?" she asked, pursing her lips and looking thoughtful. "Where did you hear a fancy name like that?"

"Oh, I don't know. I mean, I didn't say I'd heard it. What I mean is, I just wondered if you ever heard a name like it." I was feeling mighty guilty all of a sudden, with Aunt Ester sitting there staring over her glasses at me.

"It's French, I believe. Leastways, it sounds French. It has a ring to it like a dance-hall girl's name."

I swallered and blinked my eyes. "A . . . a dance-hall girl's name?"

"Over to Tylersville they have some bad places. Dance-hall places where all kinds of loose women with all kinds of fancy made-up names work. Fleur . . . hum . . . yes, it do sound like a name a feller might hear around a dance hall."

A dance hall. . . . I stared back down through the little hole at the flame of licking fire. Fleur . . . a dance-hall woman . . . a woman who couldn't keep a baby because the owner of the place didn't allow women to have babies . . . maybe he told her she couldn't dance and take care of a little baby . . . maybe *he* was the man's voice at the pond telling the woman named Fleur to leave the baby. Maybe he told her . . . I yawned and Aunt Ester took the cup of tea out of my hand.

"Off to bed with you, boy," Aunt Ester said. "You'll never beat the sun up iffen you stay up any longer."

"I don't want to beat the sun up, Aunt Ester," I told her, yawning again and standing up and tugging the Choctaw Indian blanket around me.

"You'll have to, boy. Tomorrow is Sunday and there's a mess of chores to be done before we go to church."

I went off to bed thinking about the dance-hall girls in the bad places kicking up their legs and singing loud, wild songs and a man's voice saying gruffly, "Aw, come on, Fleur. It won't do no good to cry . . ." It sure set up an ache and a pain inside me, wondering about that Fleur woman. Seemed like I could still hear her sobs just the way they sounded at the pond. I had to force myself not to think about the sound of it. I turned and looked at my mama's picture on the table beside my bed. I only know her from that picture and from what Aunt Ester has told me about her. Bear would never talk about her. Aunt Ester said it was too painful for him.

Aunt Ester said my mama looked like as if she was an angel with her hair long and golden and her smile soft and kind just like in the picture she give me. I went to sleep every night with my mama's face before my eyes. Sometimes I tried to talk to her, to tell her I wished she was here with me and how I wished she could be with Bear so he wouldn't be so lonely and always going off to places like Texas and Mexico and never settling down the way Aunt Ester said he should. Sometimes I asked her questions too, but she never answered. She just looked at me with that angel smile on her beautiful face, just like in the picture.

4
That Gut-Gnawing Worm Called Fear

The next morning, it being Sunday, I had to get up extry early and get the hay into the horses' stalls and get them fed before I could go to church. My favorite horse is Miss Pitty-Pat, the mother of Rhett and Scarlett. Aunt Ester give them those names after she read a big book about the Civil War. Miss Pitty-Pat was really old and couldn't do much of anything except stand around out in the pasture and stare forlornly at everything. Uncle Clayborn said, at her age, you couldn't expect much else. But I loved her because she was so gentle. Sometimes I'd get on her back, and she'd just stand there and never move a muscle. Or I'd talk to her real soft, and she'd raise her head back and look at me and whinny just like she understood every word I was saying.

I guess I told Miss Pitty-Pat more than I've ever told any human being, even Justin, who I tell just about everything to. I told Miss Pitty-

Pat about Bear and my mama and about how Sylvie was always hounding me about things like "true love" and holding hands and such as that. I even told Miss Pitty-Pat that sometimes Sylvie made me plumb sick to my stomach, and I'd never tell Justin that. But that morning mostly I told her about Adeline and the baby and about how I wondered who Fleur was.

When I finished getting the horses fed and was ready to leave the barn, I could hear Aunt Ester starting up the Chevy. I knew when I heard the engine turn over and grumble that I'd better get a move on. I tore out of the barn and ran around the house and jumped into the back seat of the car just in time.

"About time you got around here, boy," Aunt Ester said impatiently. "I don't know what you do all this time. There ain't nothing to feeding them horses." She took off then, down the dirt road that led away from the house and out onto the highway, kicking up dust and all the chickens that was in the path of the Chevy. Uncle Clayborn, up in the front seat beside Aunt Ester, was already snoring away with his head lopped over to one side, looking like he was dreaming about fried-chicken dinners and steaming roastin' ears.

In church I looked all around for Adeline Newberry, but I didn't see her anywhere. Once, when I was craning my neck around the front of Aunt Ester, she reached out, grabbed my ear, and hissed, "Stop that gandering around, boy!"

After church let out, Aunt Ester did some gandering around of her own, and said, "I wonder why Adeline didn't come to church today? I wonder if she's took sick? I'll have to go down to her place and have a look-see."

Justin come up to me just as we started across the churchyard and just as Zooie Marshall grabbed Aunt Ester's arm and started telling her about the latest gossip she'd heard.

Then Sylvie and Taffy Marshall come walking up.

"*That big old windstorm* didn't come today," I said, looking at Sylvie and Justin, then up into the sky.

"Oh? Oh, yeah," Justin said, catching on. "*It* sure didn't come."

"What windstorm?" Taffy asked, gazing up into the sky. "I didn't hear nothing about no windstorm coming."

I give Sylvie a look while Taffy's eyes was up in the sky, and Sylvie's mouth fell open like she just then knew what I meant.

"Oh . . . oh, I heard about it too," she said quickly. "I was wondering why *it* didn't come."

Taffy looked down from the sky and frowned. "What are y'all guys talking about? I ain't never seen such a clear sky." She looked at Sylvie and said, "Why don't you come home with me, Sylvie? I'll show you my new doll dress I made on my mama's Singer, and I'll show you the doll from Ireland I got in my collection. She's got a pretty green skirt — "

"I done seen that old doll!" Sylvie snapped.

"Shoo away now, children! Lyon has got to get home and eat his dinner," Aunt Ester said, coming up behind us.

"That's all right, ma'am," Taffy spoke up. "We got to go too. I sewed a new doll dress on my mama's Singer and Sylvie can't wait to see it. Can you, Sylvie?"

"I got more important things to think about than an old doll dress!" Sylvie blasted with a disgusted look at Taffy.

I was glad when Aunt Ester reached out and give Taffy an affectionate touch under her chin, then turned to me and said, "Come along, Lyon."

I follered Aunt Ester to the Chevy, where Uncle Clayborn was already seated and looking like he was about ready to fall asleep and go back to that chicken-and-roastin'-ears dream again. His head was nodding to the side and his eyes was fluttering closed.

When we got to the car, Aunt Ester said cantankerously, "Can't you wait until we get on the road before you start that blamed snoozin' and snorin'?"

Uncle Clayborn raised his head with a jerk and asked, "What? What did you say, Essie?"

We drove away from the church with a bounce and jolt and Aunt Ester mumbling, "I just don't know what to make of Adeline not being in church today."

I swallered hard and shrunk up into a corner of the seat and tried not to look at Aunt Ester all the way home.

When we got home, Aunt Ester bustled around getting the fried chicken and mashed pertaters and gravy on the table. When she called time for dinner and we all set down to eat, I asked her if I could go to Adeline's with her. I was itchin' inside and out to find out about the baby. It was mighty strange for Adeline not to be in church. She hardly never missed a Sunday, so I knew it had to be because of the baby.

"No, boy," Aunt Ester said, "I'll go to Adeline's alone."

"You'd best stay here and get that barn cleaned out," Uncle Clayborn said as he reached for another piece of chicken. "Miss Pitty-Pat and her young'uns will be kicking up a fuss if it ain't cleaned out right soon."

"I'll do it this evening. Uncle Clayborn," I told him.

"You'll have to do it after dinner, Lyon. The young people's meeting is tonight and it's here at the house," Aunt Ester said, and she added, "You'd best be on your Sunday behavior, boy, if you don't want to clean out the pig pen next."

I was as nervous as a squirrel salting away nuts for the winter all through the young people's meeting, wondering what Aunt Ester's reaction to the baby at Adeline's would be. But me and Justin and Sylvie didn't have a chance to talk about it because Fulton Kramer got up and went to testifying. Fulton had two missing front teeth that had been knocked out in a fight and a big crooked nose that got broken once. In some fight maybe. He was a new Christian and was always rattling off about the Bible and getting kids saved. The thing was, though, it was too easy to laugh at Fulton. If he hadn't been so funny-looking, with his knocked-out teeth and crooked nose, everyone would of took him more to heart in what he said.

Anyway, Fulton started telling about his experiences of being a Christian and how he stopped smoking out behind his barn and stopped riding up and down the street in his daddy's pickup truck looking for girls to flirt with and give rides to. He said that he'd decided the best girls was right there in the church, right under his nose every Sunday morning.

I looked at Sylvie and Taffy when Fulton said the part about the best girls being in church. They was sitting cross-legged on the floor with their shoulders hunched over and their chins pointed toward Fulton. Sylvie was like her name, all silvery, shining, and shimmering, with hair almost as white as the whitest summer clouds. Her skin was pale and she never turned brown in the summer. Taffy got her name because she was born on a night when her mama and daddy had a big taffy-pull at their house. It didn't matter none to them that her name didn't fit her coloring. Her mama tied her dark hair up in one long braid in the back. Taffy had dark eyes that reminded me of the pond when it was spinning with raindrops and getting deeper and deeper all the time, so deep that, if you jumped in, you'd go down, down, and never find your way back to the top. That's the way I felt sometimes when I looked into Taffy's eyes. Like, if I didn't look away fast, I'd get caught in them and never get out. Taffy looked like she was in a hypnotized trance listening to Fulton speak.

"If there's any one of you here that is in doubt about which way to go," Fulton said, looking hang-dog serious, "just get in a closet and ask the good Lord for guidance. He'll not let you down. I'm here to tell you that right now."

Justin jabbed me in my rib and let out a little snicker, making fun of Fulton. All over the room kids was snickering and poking at each other.

When Fulton set down, Miss Benson stood up and led us in singing "The B-i-b-l-e, Yes, That's the Book for Me." Miss Benson was Taffy's voice teacher and the church choirmistress and young people's leader. She had a little house in town with a sign out in front that said she give lessons. She had a boyfriend over to Tylersville that she said she was going to marry as soon as he made enough money.

We sang a few more songs and Miss Benson sang a solo and after that we had refreshments, cupcakes and hot cocoa and peanut-butter cookies that Aunt Ester had baked. While everyone was busy getting things out of the kitchen, I nudged Justin and whispered, "Did you hear anything yet?"

"Uh-uh. Aunt Ester's gone over to Adeline's and — "

"What are you two whispering about?" Taffy asked, moving in beside us with a cup of cocoa and some cookies on a saucer. "You're acting like conspirators."

"Aw, I bet you don't even know what that word means! You just heard it somewhere," Justin said with a sneer.

"I do too!" Taffy snapped angrily.

"What does it mean, then?"

"Why . . . why, look it up in the dictionary," Taffy said with a scowl. "If you read as much as you whispered, you'd be as smart as me!"

"I *am* as smart as you!"

"You and who else, Justin Bogart!" Taffy asked, eyeing Justin defiantly through her deep dark eyes.

"Me!" I spoke up.

"Ha. Ha. Tell me another one!" Taffy said and she flipped around and sashayed across the room to Sylvie and some other girls and, soon as she set down, they all stuck their heads together, looked over at me and Justin, and started giggling to beat sixty.

"You know, Lyon, sometimes I like Taffy a lot and sometimes I just plain can't stand her, like tonight. Fact of the matter is, I'd like to punch Taffy right in her little snout!" Justin said, sounding fuming mad and looking it too. But I knowed just how he felt.

"It ain't Christian to hit a girl," I told him.

"That's more truth than poetry," a voice said from behind us. We looked around and Fulton was standing there, smiling his snaggle-toothed smile. "In fact," he went on, "it ain't Christian to hit no one."

"Then how come you got your nose broke and your teeth punched out?" Justin asked, narrowing his eyes over Fulton.

"That was before I got to be a Christian. If you'd listen to me when I talk at you, you'd know all these things," Fulton answered.

"All what things?" I asked.

"Like how hard it is to be a Christian in today's world," Fulton replied, looking down his crooked nose at me. "Everywhere a Christian looks is temptation. Someone's always wanting to get you to lie and steal and cheat. It's hard to live an upright life."

I started thinking while Fulton was talking. Thinking about the baby and what me and Justin and Sylvie had done. It made me feel guilty like maybe I'd committed a horrible sin that could never be forgiven. It made me mad too. What right did old Fulton Kramer have making *me* feel guilty?

"What's your face turning red for?" Fulton asked sharply, and he was looking straight at me.

I swallered hard and tried to speak, but I couldn't get any words out.

"You done a sin, ain't you, Lyon Savage," Fulton went on with a pleased smile, like he was proud to know there was other sinners in the world besides hisself. I glanced at Justin. He was staring down at the floor. "I can tell every time," Fulton went on proudly. "What you done, Lyon, that you're so ashamed of? Come on, you can fess up. It'll do your soul good."

"I . . . I ain't done nothing!" I stammered, feeling my face getting hotter.

"Yes, you have. I can tell every time," Fulton accused.

Next thing I knew, Taffy was standing beside Fulton, glaring down at me and saying, "What you done, Lyon?" There was a wicked look in her dark eyes that accused me without even knowing what I'd done or if I'd done anything.

"I said, I ain't done *nothing!* Blame it, leave me alone!" I yelled.

Miss Benson, along with just about everyone else in the room, heard me and come up real quick and asked, "What is the matter, Lyon?"

I looked up at her with tears in my eyes that I was trying like the devil to blink back, but I couldn't say a word.

"Lyon's done something *evil*," Taffy said, and I wished I could jump up and yank that long braid right out of her head!

"He wants to be a Christian, but he don't know how," Fulton said proudly.

Miss Trudence Welch set down at Aunt Ester's pianola and started thumping away on "What a Friend We Have in Jesus" and drowned every other sound out. Some of the kids sitting around started singing the words.

"Fulton, don't you think you should mind your own business and let Lyon mind his? If he has a confession to make and wants your help, I'm sure he'll let you know," Miss Benson said.

A "confession," I thought, trembling. Why did she use *that* word?

Fulton's smile faded. "Yes, ma'am," he said. "I was only trying to bring another soul in for Jesus."

"I know you meant well," Miss Benson said, and she patted Fulton on his shoulder and that snaggle-toothed grin broke through like sunshine on a cloudy day. Then Miss Benson turned back to me. "Would you like a cup of cocoa, Lyon?"

I started to open my mouth when Sylvie appeared and said eagerly, "Oh, let me, Miss Benson. I'll get some cocoa for Lyon."

"Very well, Sylvie," Miss Benson said with a smile and a pat on my shoulder just like Fulton's. "Are you all right, Lyon?"

"Yes, ma'am," I answered, getting my voice back.

"You hear that song Miss Trudence is playing, Lyon? Listen to them words: 'Come to Jesus, come . . .'" Fulton started up again and Miss Benson reached out and pulled him to her and said, "Come along, Fulton. I have some things to discuss with you."

"Whew!" Sylvie exclaimed as soon as they was out of earshot. "I was scared to death you was going to let it slip about the baby!"

"I wouldn't do that," I told her. "Didn't I promise just like you and Justin did?"

Along about nine o'clock everyone left, and it wasn't long after that me and Uncle Clayborn heard Aunt Ester pull into the yard and slam on the brakes of the Chevy so hard that every chicken in her path cackled bloody murder as they flew out of her way.

"If this was Tylersville, that woman would get arrested in her own yard for driving like that!" Uncle Clayborn said, shaking his head.

We looked up at the same time when the front door popped open and Aunt Ester charged in, her face all white and her mouth flapping like bed sheets in a strong wind. It didn't take any second thoughts for me to realize that she'd found out about the baby.

"A baby! Lord have mercy, Clayborn, Adeline has got herself a baby!" Aunt Ester shouted excitedly, and I swallered so hard my tonsils almost went down my throat.

"Calm down, woman!" Uncle Clayborn demanded, and he stood up and grabbed Aunt Ester by her shoulders and stared into her face.

"Adeline's got a baby!" Aunt Ester kept shouting. "She's got a baby!"

"Sit down! Sit down!" Uncle Clayborn insisted, and he pulled Aunt Ester over to a chair and tried to force her down in it. But she wouldn't sit and she wouldn't calm down.

"I wouldn't of believed it in a hundred years! But Adeline's got herself a beautiful little boy!"

I sucked in my breath and bit down on my lip. So *that's* what the baby was!

"Adeline's too durned old to have a baby!" Uncle Clayborn stated with a flash of his eyes and a nod of his head.

"It's not her own, you old fool, it's a gift from God!"

I swallered again and it felt like my tonsils *did* go down my throat that time. I started coughing and I couldn't stop.

"What are you talking about?" Uncle Clayborn growled, frowning at Aunt Ester like he thought she'd gone as crazy as a loon.

"She said she opened her door Saturday night and there it was, a baby, right there on her front porch, and the wind and rain howling and pouring all around. It's an answer to her prayers, praise the Lord!" On the "Lord" Aunt Ester fell back into the chair behind her and exploded with what sounded like a loud horse-whinny sigh.

"On her front porch, you say, Essie?" Uncle Clayborn asked, looking mighty suspicious.

"It's a miracle, that's what it is," Aunt Ester rushed on in the same excited voice.

"If Adeline Newberry found a baby on her front porch, someone put it there and it wasn't the Lord that done it!" Uncle Clayborn boomed as he tapped his pipe in the palm of his hand and shook his head.

"The Lord works in mysterious ways, Clayborn Tarver!"

"Not *that* mysterious!" Uncle Clayborn said through puffs of lighting his pipe.

"Can I go to bed now?" I asked, trying to look and sound normal. But my knees was shaking so bad I wasn't sure I could even walk.

"What's this about wanting to go to bed so early, boy?" Aunt Ester asked me, looking right through me, it seemed.

"Let the boy go," Uncle Clayborn said. "Now, tell me about this so-called 'miracle baby.'"

"Go ahead on, boy," Aunt Ester told me. "And don't forget to say your prayers and thank the good Lord for giving Adeline her baby."

I swallered again and croaked, "Yes, ma'am."

"And put on another pair of socks. It's mighty cold tonight. They'll keep your toes warm," Aunt Ester called after me as I took off across the floor.

"Yes, ma'am," I croaked out again, and when I reached the doorway I turned and snuck a quick look at Aunt Ester and Uncle Clayborn.

Then I run as fast as I could to my room *with* my heart pounding to beat sixty.

Late into the night I could still hear the mumble of voices as Aunt Ester and Uncle Clayborn discussed Adeline Newberry's miracle baby. I couldn't sleep for all the guilt and fear that crawled around inside me like a big old gut-gnawing worm. We should of took that baby directly to the police station, just like Justin said we should, I kept telling myself. We should of took it there and left it, no matter what Sylvie said about mangy folks tying young'uns to beds and starving them. For sure and for certain, that's what we should of done. What would the Lord do to us for putting that baby on Adeline's porch and letting her think it was the Lord hisself that done it! Would he punish us by sending J. Edgar Hoover after us? I wondered in a panic of fear.

I heard thunder banging in the sky like bombs exploding and, from the winder across from my bed, I saw lightning streaking down through the big old pine trees. I rolled over and covered my head with my quilt and started praying real hard.

5
A Surprise Letter

By the next evening there wasn't a soul in all of Clement's Pond who didn't know about Adeline Newberry's miracle baby. When I passed her house on my way home from school, there was a big crowd out in the front yard and going in and out of her house. I put my head down and hurried as fast as I could, but it wasn't fast enough. The next thing I knew, Taffy was calling out to me from Adeline's fence.

"Lyon! Come here! Lyon! Adeline has a miracle baby!" she cried excitedly. "Come and see it!"

I turned and looked at Taffy with her head poked through a gap in Adeline's wood fence. I wanted to sink into the soft ruts in the muddy road. "I can't," I called back nervously. "I've got to get right home."

"What's wrong with you, Lyon Savage? Don't you want to see a true-to-goodness miracle baby? Ain't you curious at all?"

My throat was so dry and closed up and I felt so guilty, I could hardly look at Taffy, much less speak. When I opened my mouth, someone else's voice come out. I turned around and looked back down the road.

"Lyon! Wait up!" It was Justin, running down through the ruts and sloshing mud up onto his pants.

"If you don't want to see a miracle baby, then you don't believe in miracles!" Taffy yelled disgustedly.

When I turned back to the fence, she was marching up toward Adeline's house with her long dark braid swinging across her back. Justin reached me, breathing so hard his eyes was bulging out.

"D-did y-you hear? D-did you hear wh-what everyone is saying, Lyon?" he asked through big, heavy puffs for air.

"I heard," I told him, and glanced around to make sure no one was close by and listening.

"E-everyone is s-saying the baby is a *miracle baby!*" Justin's eyes was as big as winders. I'd never seen him looking so peculiar.

"We should of took it to the police, like you wanted to," I whispered miserably.

"It's too late now," Justin said, shaking his head.

"What are we going to do?"

"Nothing. There ain't nothing we can do."

"Except tell the truth. That it wasn't the Lord who put that little baby on Adeline's porch. It was us."

"No!" Justin said loudly, and Zooie Marshall,

Taffy's mama, who was standing in Adeline's yard, turned around and stared at us. Justin lowered his voice and whispered, "We *can't* do that!"

"But it's a pure sin to let Adeline and the whole town believe that the Lord made a miracle like that," I said, fidgeting my eyes back in Zooie's direction.

"She's happy, ain't she? The whole town is happy, ain't it? What have we done but bring happiness to Clement's Pond?" Justin argued.

I couldn't say a thing against that. In fact, I couldn't even open my mouth again.

The next Wednesday night in church it looked like the whole town had showed up. I saw people in that church who hadn't been in it for two solid years or more. Even old Ollie Cromwell, the biggest drunk in town, was there, looking red-faced and swollen with booze. When praying time come, it looked like the biggest sinners of all was the first to get down on their knees. And when Preacher Dawson requested all the unsaved to come forward and bow down their heads and ask the Lord for forgiveness for their sins, they was the first ones up the aisle. That in itself was a pure miracle.

When the "Hallelujahs," "Amens," and "Praise the Lords" started, Aunt Ester leaned closer to me and whispered, "I guess Adeline's baby has made believers out of them!"

I sunk back against the hard board of the seat and hung my head. I was so sick with fear about what the Lord might do to me that I couldn't even pray.

Adeline set right up in front of the congregation holding the baby. She had it wrapped in a beautiful blue-and-yeller crocheted shawl and didn't move her eyes off of it the whole time. I'd never seen Adeline looking so at peace, like there wasn't a thing in the world could ever rob her of her happiness now that she had that little baby.

After the service everyone converged around Adeline like she was holding the baby Jesus hisself in her arms. All the women sputtered and churned with laughter and strained their necks to get a gander of the baby's face as Adeline held the shawl away for them to see. The men kept up a clatter of "The Lord's will be done" and all kinds of awesome quotes from the Bible. It seemed like not one of them stopped to wonder about how that baby got on Adeline's porch. They just accepted that it was put there by the hands of God.

"What are you going to call him?" Zooie asked Adeline, and Adeline smiled over that little baby.

"I been thinking right smart about that and I've decided to call him Miracle."

There was little explosions of "ohs" and "ahs" all around and lots of jabbering and chuckling all at once. I felt so choked up with guilt that I started backing away from Aunt Ester and bumped right into Sylvie. There was such a horrible expression on her face that I wanted to turn and run from her, out of the church, and all the way home.

"Lyon!" she hissed, and moved even closer to me. "I've got to talk to you."

I glanced back at Aunt Ester. It looked like it would be a while before she was ready to leave. She had maneuvered up into the crowd surrounding Adeline and was closer to the baby than anyone else, trying to get a gander at that miracle baby. Uncle Clayborn was over by the pulpit talking to Preacher Dawson and several other men. It looked like he'd be occupied for a spell too.

"Let's go sit in Aunt Ester's car," I told Sylvie. It seemed like it would be the most private place around.

Sylvie followed me out of the church and to the side where the Chevy was parked in the darkness. We got into the back seat and Sylvie said, "That baby was my baby, Lyon! *My* little baby!"

I stared into Sylvie's face, but all I could see was the outline of her hair and the shadows that played over it, hiding her features. But I didn't have to see her face to know that she was upset.

"That baby belongs by rights to the one who found it! And old Adeline Newberry didn't find it! *I* did! It's not fair that *she* gets to keep that baby!"

"What are you saying, Sylvie?" My heart commenced to pounding to beat sixty.

"I'm saying the truth, Lyon. I want my baby! I told you I'd leave it at Adeline's on the night of the storm, but only on a loan."

"That baby ain't yours, Sylvie," I told her, and I started to tremble, scared to death that someone in the church might hear what she was saying.

"It is too! Don't say it ain't mine, Lyon! It ain't no miracle and you and me and Justin know it ain't. That baby is *mine* and I intend to call him Miles Standish." Sylvie blasted on, with her voice getting louder and louder.

"Listen to me, Sylvie, we decided — "

"I don't care *what* we decided, Lyon Savage! I want my little baby and I intend to have him!"

"Sylvie, you don't know what you're saying — "

"I know what I'm saying, all right!"

I started trembling even harder. I couldn't believe Sylvie was saying all them things. I cleared my throat and tried to be calm. "That baby belongs to someone named Fleur and we both know it."

"She left it, didn't she? That Fleur person left it right there at the pond where it could of died if we hadn't come along. She didn't give a durn what happened to that baby. But *I do*. It's 'finders keepers,' just like in everything else, Lyon." Now Sylvie's voice was trembling. Trembling like she was ready to cry.

"You wasn't the only one who found that baby, Sylvie. Just remember that!" I told her sharply, and I was surprised that I could even say it.

"What do you know about babies, Lyon?" she spit at me. "What would you do with it when it cried or had the colic or needed its diaper changed?"

"I didn't say *I* wanted the baby," I told her, feeling sweat pop out all over me. "I just said you wasn't the only one who found it."

"Adeline Newberry thinks she's so smart with my baby. But I'll show her a thing or two." There was so much of what Aunt Ester called "wicked venom" in Sylvie's voice that it scared me even more.

"What are you planning to do, Sylvie?" I asked her suspiciously.

"Something."

"Don't you go and hurt Adeline," I told her. "She loves that baby."

"The Lord giveth and the Lord taketh away."

Before I could say anything else, someone yelled, "Hey! You guys in there!"

Me and Sylvie jumped, we was so startled, and stared out the winder. The door opened slowly and Justin poked his head inside the car. "It's me and Taffy," he said.

I was relieved. "Get in," I told them.

They got in the back seat and set down and looked over at me and Sylvie. "What are y'all guys talking about out here?" Taffy asked.

"Just enjoying the scenery," I spoofed her.

"You must be an old hoot owl then, to see in the dark!" Taffy giggled.

"Is everyone still hanging around Adeline?" I asked them.

"Like flies to tar," Justin answered.

I could see the outline of Sylvie folding her arms over her chest. "Well, let Miss Adeline Newberry have her day!" she said, and it sounded like a threat again.

"What do you mean by that?" Taffy asked.

"That's for me to know and you to find out!" Sylvie snapped.

I didn't like the way Sylvie was talking. I was afraid she was going to tell Taffy everything and, the next thing to happen, Taffy would tell her mama, and Zooie would tell Aunt Ester, and . . . It made me sick to even think what might happen.

"You sure are in a mean mood. I bet I know why, too," Taffy said.

All of a sudden there wasn't a sound in that car. I looked at Sylvie, trying to see her face, but it was lost in the darkness. Then I looked at Justin. I couldn't see his face neither, but it seemed like they was both staring at me and had stopped breathing.

"Wh-what do y-you mean, Taffy?" Justin asked in an odd voice.

"Sylvie's jealous because I got me a new doll that's got a whole wardrobe of clothes and a suitcase to put them in and little hangers besides, and . . ." Taffy said smartly, and for the next few seconds that car fair about exploded with heavy, relieved breathing.

Then Sylvie said angrily, "I ain't jealous of no old dolls! I give up dolls before you ever started that dumb old collection of yours!"

"Ever since I showed you my new doll that Mama got me for my collection, you've mooned around like you was mad as an old hornet, Sylvie," Taffy accused.

"No old *play* doll can compare to a *real* baby!" Sylvie cried.

"What do you mean?" Taffy asked.

Justin laughed nervously. "Hey, let's drop

this stupid subject. This sure is a stupid subject."

"Yeah, it sure is that, all right," I agreed, giving out with a croaklike laugh. "I can think of lots more interesting things to talk about besides old dolls. Ain't you got a birthday coming up soon, Taffy?" I asked, hoping and praying to change the subject.

"Why, Lyon, how did you know?" Taffy asked, sounding pert and sugary. Even in the darkness of the car, I knew them dark eyes was pinned on me.

"Don't you think Lyon's got a memory?" Sylvie asked. "He's only been going to your dumb old parties for the past hundred years!"

Justin laughed nervously. I swallered hard and leaned back against the car seat. Seemed like I'd never seen such a black night. It was like us in that car was the only things in the world.

"My birthday parties ain't dumb!" Taffy cried defensively.

"How old will you be, Taffy?" Justin asked real fast, before Sylvie could jump onto Taffy again.

"I'll be twelve years old, Justin," Taffy answered like everyone should set up and take notice of that.

"Aw, to be twelve again!" I said, and croaked out another laugh.

"You try to make us think you're so old and worldly, Lyon. But you ain't," Sylvie said. "You're only thirteen."

"That's one up on you," I told her. Sylvie

wouldn't be thirteen until I turned fourteen. Justin was my age, but a few months younger.

"Shush!" Taffy said sharply. "I hear Mama calling me."

We listened. There was nothing but an old hound dog barking off in the distance.

"That ain't your mama." Justin snickered. "That's an old rooster cackling over yonder in that field."

Taffy jumped up in the seat toward Justin and raised her arm to slap him just as the car door popped open.

"Taffy Marshall, you get out of this car this very minute!" It was Zooie Marshall with a flashlight in her hand, shining it right into our faces.

"I wasn't doing nothing but talking, Mama," Taffy said in a trembling voice. In the light from the flashlight I could see her face all crumpled up and her eyes filled with fear.

"I said, get out of this car this minute!" Zooie repeated, and we could tell she meant business.

Taffy obeyed and slunk out of the car like she'd already gotten a beating. As soon as she was out, Zooie shined the flashlight right into my face and said, "Your aunt will certainly hear about this, Lyon Savage!" Then she took hold of the door and slammed it so hard the whole car shook. She didn't even pay no mind to Justin ner Sylvie. Seemed like she had it in for me.

It didn't seem like more than a minute later that Aunt Ester come up to the car and snapped open the door. "What is the meaning of this?" she demanded.

"We was just talking, Aunt Ester," I told her in a feeble, shaking voice.

"Sylvie, you get along now with your brother," Aunt Ester said sternly, and Justin and Sylvie climbed out of the car and run around the corner of the church, almost bumping smack-dab into Uncle Clayborn as he come ambling around from the other side.

"What's all this nonsense about you young'uns dilly-dallying around in the car tonight?" Uncle Clayborn asked me as we drove home.

"We wasn't dilly-dallying, Uncle Clayborn," I told him, feeling embarrassed enough to flat out die. "We was only talking."

"In the dark, in the car, with the doors closed and the winders all up!" Aunt Ester snorted accusingly.

"It was cold," I reminded her.

"If you wasn't dilly-dallying and you was only talking, what was you talking about that you couldn't do it inside the church or in front where the light is?" Aunt Ester asked, like she was old J. Edgar Hoover hisself and giving me the third degree.

"It wasn't nothing important that you'd be interested in, Aunt Ester," I said glumly as I stared out the car winder and watched the low, flat fields go by like a black blur.

"Oh, I see. It was politics and such as that!" Aunt Ester said as we swung into the yard and almost hit the porch post.

"We was just talking about Taffy's birthday party," I told her as a chicken landed on the hood of the Chevy, cackling wildly.

I hadn't exactly lied to Aunt Ester. We was talking about Taffy's birthday, too. I sure wasn't about to tell her and Uncle Clayborn about the miracle baby that wasn't a miracle at all!

Just as I was settling down for bed, Uncle Clayborn come into my room and said in a low voice, "Don't worry, Lyon. I know you wasn't doing nothing wrong tonight. I'll put in a word for you with your Aunt Essie."

"Thanks, Uncle Clayborn," I told him gratefully, and snuggled down under my quilt.

After I was in bed awhile and trying to concentrate on my mama, Aunt Ester come in and said like she wasn't mad anymore, "I reckon you won't be getting no invite to Taffy's birthday party this year, Lyon. Zooie had a hissy-fit over tonight. You know how she is about Taffy."

"But we wasn't doing nothing wrong. Honest, Aunt Ester. Zooie shouldn't of acted like we was."

"Zooie won't believe a thing she don't want to believe. But I'll take her down some preserves in a day or two and see if I can set things right. You got to be mighty careful about some girls, Lyon. Especially when they have a mama like Zooie Marshall. It brings a bitterness into a woman like Zooie, to be left with no man and a child to raise. But your daddy can tell you all about such things, I suppose. And, speaking of your daddy . . ." Aunt Ester stopped and smiled at me, ". . . he's coming home."

I set up in bed like a wild wind had hurled me out of a cave. Bear was coming back! "Why didn't you tell me, Aunt Ester?" I demanded. "Why didn't you tell me?"

She chuckled. "Well, I just did, boy."

"I mean, before. Why didn't you tell me earlier?"

"George Goad just give me the letter tonight in church. With all the excitement over Adeline's baby and Zooie acting up, I just plain forgot about it. But here's the letter. You can read it for yourself." She pulled an envelope out of her pocket and handed it to me. "Don't strain your eyes, now. Go over by the lamp."

I grabbed the letter, jumped out of bed, and rushed to the table where the lamp sat. I pulled the letter out of the envelope and read it with such interest that I didn't even know when Aunt Ester left the room.

"Hello, everyone . . . and a special hello to you, Lyon," the letter started off. "I'm planning to leave here on the tenth of next month and hope to be in Clement's Pond before the roads are dried out good. I won't be able to stay long, as I am going up to Alaska with a feller I've made a quick acquaintance with here. He has a piece of property there and needs a partner to help him fell some trees and tame some wild horses. He thinks I'd make a good foreman and I do too. So, that's where I'll be headed when I leave Clement's Pond . . ."

I read the letter four whole times all the way through, until I practically knew every word by heart. When I finally put it back into the envelope and turned out the lamp it must have been very late because the only sound in the house was Uncle Clayborn and Aunt Ester snoring in unison.

Bear coming home ... I could hardly wait! I snuggled down into my covers and thought of Mama and wished she could be there waiting for Bear to come home along with me. Only thing was, though, it seemed like Bear was already talking about leaving before he'd even come back. Looked like things never was going to change in that department.

6
I Make Up My Mind About Something Big

The definition of a miracle, the dictionary said, is "An act or event that seems to transcend or contradict all known or scientific laws and is usually thought to be supernatural in origin. Any wonderful or amazing thing, fact or event; a wonder."

"A wonder . . . that's what folks think Adeline's baby is," I said out loud as I stared through the winder out at the pasture where Miss Pitty-Pat stood stone-still, gazing off at nothing, it seemed like. "A wonderful or amazing thing . . . supernatural . . ."

"What are you doing, boy, sitting in here talking to yourself?" Aunt Ester's voice shot across the room at me and I jumped. She laughed and said, "What's in that book there?"

I snapped the pages of the dictionary closed and stood up. "Did you want something, Aunt Ester?" I asked her nervously. "I been meaning to clean out Miss Pitty-Pat's stall . . ."

"That can wait," she said, and she come over to the table and looked down at the dictionary. "A boy that studies his books is bound to go far in the world. Your daddy will be proud to know your mind is set to book learning."

"Yes, ma'am," I said, trying not to look guilty. Seems like I was always trying not to look guilty, ever since we put the baby on Adeline's porch.

"It being Saturday, I reckon you'll be wanting to go over to the Bogarts' and fool around with Justin," Aunt Ester said as she started out of the room.

"I guess I better do Miss Pitty-Pat's stall first," I told her.

"Suit yourself, boy," she said as she left the doorway.

It wasn't that I didn't want to go to see Justin. It wasn't even that I didn't want to go to his house. I really liked his mama and daddy and all that. And I sure didn't want to clean out Miss Pitty-Pat's stall when I could be out fooling around and having a good time. But, the truth of the matter was, I didn't want to see Sylvie. I kept thinking about what she'd said about that little baby being hers and how I promised to be her true love and it give me goose prickles just to remember. I didn't know what Sylvie might be up to and it worried me night and day.

In the barn I got the shovel and started scraping up the manure from Miss Pitty-Pat's stall and carrying it around to the side of the barn. "I wish you had to do this, Miss Pitty-Pat," I told her. "Then you'd know what work is. Only work you ever did was to stand around in the pasture swishing your tail at butterflies and watching Aunt Ester's wash blow in the wind."

Miss Pitty-Pat lifted her nose and stared at me like I was the old hunchback Gypsy and she couldn't stand looking at me for saying what I did. I laughed and patted her gently on her head. "It's okay, Miss Pitty-Pat," I told her. "I didn't mean to hurt your feelings."

I heaved the last of the manure up into the shovel and took it around the barn, then I put some fresh straw in Miss Pitty-Pat's stall and put feed in a bucket for her. While she was pushing the bucket around with her nose, I went out of the barn and perched up on the corral fence and looked up into the sky. It glittered with the brightness of spring and sunshine. Not a cloud sailed in the blue. It would be a good day for Bear to come home, I thought.

It had been six months or more since I'd seen Bear. Six months was the shortest time he'd ever stayed away. Usually it was more than a year. And sometimes when he come back, I didn't even know him. It would be the same hairy-faced, bearded Bear, with hulking shoulders and chest and long, thick legs and a laugh that could be heard from Clement's Pond all the way to Tylersville and the Jenkins county line. But sometimes I didn't know how to act, he'd been away so long.

Bear was always jolly and acted like he'd never been away more than an hour or two. He never acted like we was strangers and he greeted everyone like he'd just stepped around the corner for a minute. I reckon everyone in Clement's Pond liked Bear except Zooie Marshall, who acted mighty peculiar when he was around. It looked like sometimes she liked him a whole lot and other times like she plumb hated him.

While I sat on that corral fence looking up into the sky, I made up my mind I was going to ask Bear to stay this time, stay and not go away again. Not go to Alaska with his friend, but stay here in Clement's Pond with me and Aunt Ester and Uncle Clayborn. I made up my mind what I was going to say to Aunt Ester when she asked me what I was going to say when Bear come home. I knew she would ask. She always did.

"What are you going to say to Bear when he comes home, Lyon?" Aunt Ester asked me at the supper table that night.

"I'm going to tell him that if he don't stay here with me, I'm going to go to Alaska with him," I answered.

"Now, you know you ain't going to do that," Aunt Ester said as she handed me the platter of hot biscuits. "This is your home and you know you couldn't go away and leave it, even if Bear did want to take you with him."

"Which he won't," Uncle Clayborn said from a mouth filled up with turnip greens.

"Maybe he will," I said stubbornly.

"All your friends are here," Aunt Ester said, studying me over the top of her glasses.

"Bear can't settle long enough to take care of a boy like you," Uncle Clayborn said.

"I'm older now. I'm thirteen. I can take care of myself practically," I said, shoving out my thin-as-a-bone chest.

"Practically!" Uncle Clayborn snorted and reached for the platter with the biscuits on it.

"What would you do out there in Alaska?" Aunt Ester asked, frowning at me.

"Well, I'd ... I could ..."

"Never go to school, that's what," Uncle Clayborn said, smacking his lips over a buttery biscuit.

I turned a scowl on him. "Yes, I would too!"

"Roaming around the country ain't the life, boy. You got to wake up to that fact right now. Bear will tell you. Even he will tell you that," Aunt Ester said gravely.

"If you ask him," Uncle Clayborn said, munching away.

"Well ... well, I *will* ask him. I will!" I blasted and, all at once, my voice was trembling and so were my knees and hands. I tried to pick up my glass of milk but my fingers touched it the wrong way and the glass toppled over and spilled all over Aunt Ester's tablecloth and into the bowl of mashed pertaters.

"Never mind that, boy," Aunt Ester said gently, standing up and heading for the sink to get a rag to wipe up the milk with.

I started trembling even more and when I couldn't stand it another minute, I jumped up and run from the table to my room.

"Where are you going, Lyon?" Uncle Clayborn boomed.

"Leave him be," Aunt Ester said. "Leave the

boy be. Can't you see he's all atremble over his daddy coming home?"

A little later, lying across my bed, I could hear Aunt Ester and Uncle Clayborn talking. Their voices was low and I knew they didn't want me to hear what they was saying and it wasn't that I even wanted to hear. It was like Aunt Ester said: even standing out on the porch, you could hear a moth fall in the back of the house. That's how thin the walls was.

"The boy is homesick for his daddy," Aunt Ester said. "I can see it now like I never been able to see it before."

"Won't do him no good. Bear won't settle. Never will," Uncle Clayborn said.

"Oh, if only Theola hadn't passed away," Aunt Ester sighed. "If only she had lived and could of been a mother to that boy and a wife to Bear just a little longer." She stopped and sighed again, and it was the lonesomest sound I'd ever heard just about. It was like a heavy wind blowing down through the pine trees in back of the house and the sky all split apart and the chickens flying across the yard and Miss Pitty-Pat standing and looking forlornly at the raindrops on the ground while they fell all around her. It was sad and lonely and like a bad storm brewing that wouldn't go away. I shivered just to think about it, and pulled the Choctaw Indian blanket up over me.

"Bear should of stopped pining over Theola after all these years," Uncle Clayborn said, and I could tell from the way he talked that he was lighting his pipe.

"I suppose . . . I suppose . . ." Aunt Ester said forlornly.

"He should of met someone else and got married again."

"He couldn't, Clayborn. He just couldn't. You know that."

"There has always been plenty of women around who would of been glad to marry Bear Savage."

"Bear wouldn't have the best of them. Not the best or the grandest. Not after Theola."

I fell asleep to the sound of their voices rising and falling throughout the house and, late into the night, I woke up and crawled under the covers with all my clothes on and snuggled down, thinking about my mama and Bear.

7
A Promise
and a Commitment

A few days later, I was out behind the henhouse whittling a stick into a spear for the next time I went froggin', when I heard a strange sound. It was sort of like the excited, painful yell of a person being splashed with icy cold water. It was high and quivery and low and husky at the same time and so loud it sounded like an echo bouncing back and forth all across the valley. It was sort of all that. But it was more, too. It was familiar. That's what it was about that weird sound.

"Geeeechaaaaaaaa!"

I dropped the whittling stick and started running.

"Geeeeehaaaaaaaa!"

I ran to the road and looked up and down. Out of the edge of my eye I saw Aunt Ester fly down the porch steps wiping her hands on her long apron and charge out behind me. Uncle

Clayborn ran in from the field and yelled, "It's him! It's Bear."

"Oh, Lordy, it's Bear come home!" Aunt Ester cried excitedly when she reached me.

Bear! Bear come home! I kept thinking over and over while my breath blew in and out of me in quick, short spurts. Bear's home!

Up and down the road we could see people coming out on their porches, looking all around, wondering what the peculiar noise was. But by the next wild "Geeeeehaaaaaaa!" they knew. No one had seen him yet, but we could all hear him.

"It's Bear Savage, ain't it?" someone shouted, and Uncle Clayborn shouted back, "It's Bear, all right!"

"Bear's come home!"

"Bear Savage is back!"

"Bear Savage!"

People left their porches and ran to meet each other at the edge of the road, watching in the direction of where the yelling come from. I was so excited I was shaking all over and my mouth was as dry as the dust Rhett and Scarlett kicked up in the back field on a hot summer's day. I looked and looked, but still Bear wasn't in view.

"Geeeeehaaaaaaa!"

It come again and I was getting ready. I could feel my feet trembling in my brogans, getting ready the minute I caught sight of Bear, to take off running in his direction.

"Geeeeehaaaaaaa!"

He was there all of a sudden, less than half a mile away, walking up the road in that wide stride and brisk step that Aunt Ester said was all Bear's own. He was walking and laughing and yelling and it come to me as I watched him, like music from some opera I never heard but could imagine coming from the opera house over to Tylersville. He was walking and getting closer.

"There he is!" someone yelled.

I glanced up at Aunt Ester. "Go on, boy," she said with a gentle smile. "Run to your daddy."

I took off down the road like all my clothes had caught on fire and the only way to put it out was to run as fast as I could. And that's the way I felt inside, too. Like my whole insides was about to explode with a fiery happiness and the only way to keep from dying was to keep running and running until . . .

I fell into Bear's arms and he lifted me high above his head like I was some little old hummingbird that didn't weigh an ounce and like I wasn't thirteen years old. I was nothing but a feather to Bear. He was so big and so strong, he could lift a plow horse without any trouble! When he set me down, he bent to one knee and looked into my face like he was studying me real hard.

"Hello, Lyon Savage," he said. "How you be, boy?"

I threw my arms around Bear's neck and he hugged me to him and we held on to each other like we was glued tight. I tried not to cry. I tried not even to sniffle, but a tear fell out and ran down my nose and I had to sniffle to keep all the rest from coming out and rolling down my face. Suddenly Bear put his arm around my shoulders and started walking with me while he laughed and talked and greeted everyone standing along the road.

"How long you staying this time, Bear?" someone asked.

"Till I leave," Bear answered, and everyone laughed.

"Where you been, Bear?" someone else called out.

"Everywhere," Bear answered, and they laughed again.

All the way to the end of the road people was calling out, "Good to see you, Bear!" "Glad you're back, Bear!"

When we reached the yard, Bear pulled Aunt Ester into his arms and kissed her right on her lips.

"You're home, Bear," Aunt Ester whispered. "Home where you belong."

When Bear released Aunt Ester, he reached out and hugged Uncle Clayborn and Uncle Clayborn brushed a sniffle from under his nose and said, "Dogged if it ain't good to see you, Bear."

Bear turned and waved to everyone standing along the road before the four of us walked into the yard and up to the house. When we got inside, Bear looked at me and said, "Now let me get a good gander at you, Lyon Savage."

He gandered me, all right, up and down, all the way from my dark hair and brown eyes to the tips of my old leather brogans, the Army boots Uncle Clayborn give me. All the time he was looking, I was thinking: Maybe he don't like the way I look ... maybe he thinks I'm too skinny, not big like he is ... maybe he thinks I look sissyfied because my bones is small and my arms is long and ...

"God, I'm proud of you, boy!" Bear said and he grabbed me to him and hugged me longer and harder than he ever had and all my fears went out of me.

When Bear let me go he kept studying me and I pushed a tear away from my eye with the tip of my finger and said, "I sure did miss you, Bear. I sure did."

"Bear, come and eat!" Aunt Ester called out from the kitchen. "I been fixing special things every day, thinking you'd come. There ain't hardly a speck of room on the counter for all the pies and cakes and sweet rolls lined up!"

Bear chuckled. His chuckle was warm and merry-sounding and it made his dark eyes twinkle like he had a good secret hid somewhere behind them. There was no one in the world like Bear. No one nowheres.

In my room that night while Bear sat in a chair pulling off his boots, I asked him, "Will you stay this time, Bear?" I was sitting up in bed watching him, hoping he'd look up and say what I wanted to hear. But he just kept unlacing his boots and pulling them off. "Did you hear me, Bear?" I asked, frowning over him.

Bear let the second boot drop to the floor and looked up at me. "I heard what you said, Lyon."

"What's your answer? Will you stay and

never go away from Clement's Pond again?" I asked eagerly. If only Bear would stay!

"No, boy. I can't say that."

"Why?" I cried, and I could feel a storm brewing in me.

"I'm committed, boy. I'm going to Alaska."

"What do you mean, 'committed'?" I studied Bear's face hard, wishing I'd never see him walk up the road away from me again.

"I've got a job waiting for me. I promised — "

"Committed and promised and I don't care!"

"Here now, boy!" Bear said and he come to the bed and sat down on the edge of it and put his arm around me. "You get spoiled while I been away this time? Is that it?" he asked me.

"No, sir," I answered, looking fiercely at him and shaking my head. "It ain't that."

"Then, tell me what it is."

"It's that everyone around here has a daddy at home but me! It's that they have a daddy to talk to and be with and do things with and I don't! I'm like I don't belong because I ain't got a daddy..."

"You've got a daddy, Lyon."

"I mean, you ain't *here!* I can't ever see you ner go fishing with you ner anything. Don't you see what I mean, Bear?" I was staring into Bear's eyes, wishing that he'd suddenly say he was ready to stay and never go away again.

"Some things can't be, son," he said, and he touched my cheek with his rough-feeling hand. "Some things are hard on us, but we just have to take them in our stride."

"Like Mama dying?" I asked, watching Bear's face for the flicker of pain that was always there whenever Mama was mentioned.

Bear moved his hand away. "Yes. Like your mama dying," he said softly.

"But that couldn't be helped," I told him. "You going or staying here *can* be helped. You could stay if you wanted to."

"What if I promised you I'd come home oftener than I used to? What if I promised I'd come every six months? What about that? You can see I'm here sooner this time than I have been in years. Time goes by fast."

"Do you mean, it would be a commitment? A commitment, like you made to the man who wants to go to Alaska?" I asked, looking at Bear with pain in my eyes and in my chest and all over me.

"Yes, Lyon. A promise and a commitment. Between father and son."

"Words!" I blasted.

"Them two words is mighty important, Lyon. If I was away and your Aunt Ester took down sick, you'd help take care of her, wouldn't you? You'd see she got her herb tea and you'd read her favorite verses to her from the Bible, wouldn't you? You'd do all of that before you went off, wouldn't you?"

"Yes, sir."

"Well, that's sort of a commitment. It's something you got to do before you do anything else. Do you see what I mean?"

"I guess so." I put my head down and sulked

while I spoke. Bear wasn't saying anything I wanted to hear. He wasn't saying he would stay or even think about staying.

"Chin up, boy," he said as he lifted my chin with his fingers.

I had to smile. I had to because I didn't want Bear to be mad at me or to think I was some kind of sissyfied baby.

Bear stood up, pulled off his clothes, and said, "Move over, boy, and let me crawl in. It's cold out here." I made room for him and he scooted under the covers beside me.

"Still say your prayers, boy?" Bear asked as he pulled the covers up.

"Yes, sir," I told him.

"Then say a special one for your mama. Say one so she'll know what a fine son she's got growing up down here on this old earth. Will you do that, Lyon?"

I said I would and I did. And I said even an extry-special one for Bear because I loved him so much.

After a while when the night sounds settled down, I said into the darkness, "Know what, Bear?"

"What?" Bear asked and I could tell he was almost asleep.

"Miss Adeline Newberry's got a baby." I held my breath and sunk my teeth into my bottom lip, afraid I'd spill everything all out if I wasn't careful. My eyes groped in the dark room for Mama's picture that sat on the table beside my bed, but I couldn't see it.

"That's fine," Bear said sleepily.

"It's a . . . a miracle baby."

"A *what!*" Bear sounded wide-awake all of a sudden.

"Adeline named it Miracle and she said it was a miracle baby," I went on, like as if I didn't have a guilty conscience ner nothing.

"A miracle baby, huh?" Bear snorted into loud chuckles.

"Yes, sir," I answered, but my words almost got lost in my swaller.

"Where did that miracle baby come from?"

"Her front porch." My heart like to have beat right out of my chest in that moment.

"*What?*" Bear sat up and leaned on his elbow. It was dark but I knew he was staring down at me. Light from the winder across the room behind him made his form look immense.

"On her f-front p-porch," I repeated.

"How in the name of wild Indians did a baby get on Adeline Newberry's front porch?"

"Well, sir . . ." I stopped and gulped. Why did Bear have to ask me that? Why did I ever bring it up in the first place? I wondered miserably. "Well, sir . . ." I started again, "she opened her door and there it was."

It wasn't exactly a lie, I tried to tell myself. Leastways, not a lie to hurt nobody. But I purely expected to have big fat warts on my tongue the next morning. That's what happened to kids who told lies, according to Aunt Ester.

Bear lay back and started laughing. "Geeehaaa! Adeline Newberry with a 'miracle' baby that she found on her front porch! Now, you don't believe that, do you, son? You don't believe it was a miracle that put that baby there, do you?"

I swallered one of them swallers that near about took my tonsils down my throat and said, "The whole town believes it."

"I've got to get a gander at that miracle baby. Geeehaaa!" Bear laughed again and turned over and soon started snoring.

8
Zooie Marshall
Strikes Again

I laid awake for a long time listening to Bear and Aunt Ester and Uncle Clayborn all three snoring. It seemed like dawn was exploding over the valley and the sun was already on its way up before I closed my eyes. And it seemed like I no sooner got them closed before the rooster was crowing and Aunt Ester was knocking on the door and telling me it was time to get up and get ready for school. Bear was still asleep, so I crept out of bed as quietly as I could and got dressed without even turning on the lamp.

At the breakfast table I told Aunt Ester, "I wish I could stay home today. Bear's first day home, I sure would like to."

"No," Aunt Ester said emphatically. "Bear wouldn't want that. And I don't want it neither. If I let you stay home today, you'll just want to stay home tomorrow, and the next thing we know, we'll have a dunce on our hands. Now, we don't want that, do we?" She stared at me over the top of her glasses and, without waiting for me to answer, she went right on talking. "Of course we don't. Miss Hobson would have a pure fit and the truant officer would be out here reading me the law in no uncertain terms. Why, he might even call in J. Edgar Hoover hisself! You wouldn't want that, now, would you, boy?" She stopped what she was doing at the sink and turned around and give me an over-the-glasses look again. "You eat them biscuits and honey and get down the road to the bus stop."

At the mention of J. Edgar Hoover's name, my mouth went completely dry and I started shaking. The biscuit fell between my fingers and landed in the blob of golden honey in my plate. I looked up at Aunt Ester. She had turned back to the sink and was humming. I picked up my schoolbooks and the sack of lunch beside my plate and told Aunt Ester good-bye, hoping there wasn't any difference in the sound of my voice. I guess there wasn't, because Aunt Ester said good-bye in her usual way and I went out the door.

I walked down the road wishing I could take back that night when me and Justin and Sylvie went froggin' at the pond. I wished I could take it back and do the whole durned day over. J. Edgar Hoover . . . the FBI strikes again! I could hear just the way they'd announce it over the radio. I could hear me and Justin and Sylvie's names being said like as if we was the most-wanted criminals in America. Worse even than Bonnie and Clyde and Pretty Boy Floyd and all them crooks. By the time I reached the bus stop, I was broke out in a pure sweat of nerves.

"Ain't you glad Bear is home?" Sylvie asked, and I looked up from the road where my eyes had been from the house to the bus stop. Justin and Taffy was standing beside her with their books and sack lunches in their hands, waiting for the bus.

"You bet," I said. What a stupid question, I thought. Who wouldn't be glad to have their very own daddy with them?

"You reckon Bear will stay a spell?" Justin asked.

I shrugged, thinking of Bear's "commitment."

"My mama says Bear won't stay any longer than he has to!" Taffy said, tossing her long braid over her shoulder and squeezing her schoolbooks up tight and staring at me sideways of her eyes.

"I ain't never heard of no one as rude as you, Taffy!" Sylvie scolded.

"I am not rude! Do you think I'm rude, Lyon?" Taffy asked, looking at me from out of hurt eyes. "All I'm saying is the pure truth. My mama says Bear Savage never done a thing for Lyon! Not a thing but come and go all his life!"

"Aw, shut up, Taffy," Justin muttered.

"I won't shut up! And what's more, my mama said you and Lyon was trying to tempt me and Sylvie that night we was in Miss Ester's car at the church!"

I glared at Taffy. Sparks was flying in them black eyes. "You know that ain't true," I told her evenly.

"You'd better tell your mama that she's wrong!" Sylvie cried with her eyes narrowed into what looked like a threat.

"I did tell her. But she won't believe me. Lyon, Mama's bound and determined that she's going to have a talk with Bear about you," Taffy said with her face puckering up like she was about to cry.

"I ain't done nothing wrong," I said with a fierce passion.

"My mama don't want to believe it," Taffy said. "She says if I don't tell her the truth about what happened that night in Miss Ester's car, she'll never buy me another doll for my collection as long as I live! Them dolls is the *love of my life*, Lyon! I only got *five* and there's *seven more* left in the collection that I *ain't* got!" Taffy sniffled over the desperate sound in her voice and ran the back of her hand under her nose. You would of thought them dolls was the keys to God's kingdom, to hear Taffy tell it.

I shouldn't of, but I felt sorry for Taffy. Even more sorry than mad at her. Her mama was always onto her about some little old something that didn't amount to a chicken feather in the wind. If Taffy wasn't getting a switchin', she was getting a tongue-lashing or being accused of some dumb old something.

"Taffy Marshall, I can't believe that even you would be so stupid as to confess to something that ain't even true just to get an old doll!" Sylvie spoke up.

"Well, of course not! I'd never do a thing like that, Sylvie," Taffy said, and her lips was quivering like she was going to cry in the next second.

The bus was coming and we got on and me and Justin sat together and didn't talk to Sylvie or Taffy all the way to school. When we got off the bus, Justin whispered to me, "It ain't Taffy's fault she's got Zooie Marshall for a mother."

"I know that," I told him.

That evening, just after Aunt Ester got the supper dishes put away, Zooie come dragging Taffy up the front steps and demanded to talk to Bear.

"What on earth is on your mind, Zooie? And why are you pulling that child that way?" Aunt Ester asked, frowning at Zooie. She opened the door and Zooie charged through, yanking Taffy behind her.

"I got me plenty on my mind, Ester Tarver! Plenty! Just you call Bear out here and let me say my piece! This here is between me and Lyon's daddy. Not you," Zooie exploded at Aunt Ester and she raised her long nose in the air and snuffed in Aunt Ester's direction like Aunt Ester was the rutted ground she'd just walked off of.

I was sitting at the kitchen table doing my homework and had a good view of the front room. I leaned my head a little to the side and got a gander of Taffy standing there, looking awful, like as if she'd just had a hard walloping. Her eyes was all swollen and red-rimmed and her cheeks was puffy like she'd been crying for a long time. Bear was in the bedroom when Aunt Ester went to get him. He come out of the bedroom hitching his suspenders up over his shoulders and smiling a big friendly smile.

"Hello, Zooie," Bear said pleasantly when he saw Zooie, but Zooie cut right into him.

"I'll have you know, Bear Savage, that your son, Lyon, tried to tempt my little girl."

"Whoa!" Bear pleaded, raising his hand. "Whoa, there, Zooie! Back up about nine acres!" A frown took over where the smile left off on Bear's face.

"Tell him, Taffy! Go on, tell Lyon's daddy what Lyon done to you," Zooie urged Taffy, who looked petrified with fear. "Go on!" Zooie demanded, and her face was as red as a red cabbage.

"He . . . he . . . k-kissed . . . he kissed m-me!" Taffy cried, and mad as I was at her for lying, I still couldn't keep from feeling sorry for her.

"Geeeehaaaaa!" Bear exploded, and threw back his head and laughed so loud and hard, I don't know how the winders stayed inside the frames.

Zooie's face went from red to stark white. "What are you laughing about, Bear Savage?"

"Is *that* what you call a temptation, Zooie? You call a little innocent kiss between a normal boy and girl, *a temptation?*" Bear's eyes was two big balls bouncing over Zooie.

"Who said it was innocent?" Zooie snapped, and she looked mad enough and mean enough to strangle Bear!

"Why, the Lord have mercy!" Aunt Ester cried, looking shocked and disgusted at the same time.

"Come here, darlin'," Bear said to Taffy, and he dropped down to his knees and held his arms out. "Come here and let's talk about this."

But Zooie wouldn't let Taffy's hand go. She held it so tight that Taffy was whimpering in pain.

"Goldang it, Zooie!" Bear erupted, getting back to his feet. "If you don't let me talk to the young'un, how am I to know what happened?"

"I'm telling you what happened!" Zooie slung back at Bear.

Suddenly Bear's whole face changed like a hurricane ready to rip the place apart. "Lyon! Lyon Savage, come in here!" he thundered.

I set my pencil down and slunk out of the kitchen, walking with my shoulders all hunched over, scared to death of what was going to happen. It looked like I was acting guilty even though I wasn't.

"Did you hear what Zooie accused you of, son?" Bear asked sternly, but his eyes on me was as soft as they always was.

"Y-yes, sir," I answered right up.

"Is it the truth, Lyon?"

I swallered and glanced over at Taffy, knowing that if it was the truth or a lie, either one, Taffy would suffer. She got a licking every time she turned around. Didn't matter to her mama if she was guilty or not. Seemed like Zooie just took everything out on Taffy. But I couldn't let Bear think I'd tried to tempt her. "No, sir," I answered finally.

"Bah!" Zooie snorted, giving me a hateful, accusing look.

"You've always been taught truth and honesty in this house, ain't that a fact, boy?" Bear asked.

I swallered again. "Y-yes, sir," I said, but I couldn't keep from thinking, in that minute, about what me and Justin and Sylvie had done. I glanced around the room at everyone, wishing I was anywhere but standing there hearing Taffy whimper and feeling her mother's eyes burn into me.

Bear stepped over and put his arm on my shoulder. "I believe you, son," he said.

"And so do I," Aunt Ester said with a firm smack of her lips.

"Flitter! That boy is filling you up with hogwash! He knows what he's done!" Zooie cried, grinding in that hateful, accusing look at me. I bit into my lip and looked over at Taffy again.

"Honey," Bear said gently to Taffy, but she wouldn't look up from the floor at him. "I don't know why you told what you did, but you must think you have a mighty good reason."

Zooie started shoving Taffy toward the door. "I won't listen to you, Bear Savage! And I won't let my girl listen to you, neither! You always did have a smooth tongue. You always did know just how to sweet-talk any old silly fool girl that come along!"

What did Zooie mean by that? I wondered. Bear didn't sweet-talk no old silly fool girls that I knew of.

Zooie swung out the door pushing Taffy ahead of her. They went down the porch steps three at a time and hurried across the yard like a streak of lightning.

Bear turned me around to face him. "Why did Taffy tell that lie on you, son?" he asked, watching my face closely. His own face looked furrowed with a deep sadness.

"I don't know, Bear," I told him.

But it wasn't long after that that I found out why.

9
I See Taffy as a True Girl

"That Old Paint is a pure demon," Uncle Jack said as he leaned over the corral fence in back of his house. "A demon straight out of the red pit. There ain't no rest ner peace for it till it throws somebody."

The pinto was so far away when I'd walked up to where Uncle Jack stood watching it, that I couldn't tell who was riding it. But someone was on it and galloping like fury across the wide-open field heading toward the woods.

"Yes, sir," Uncle Jack went on with his eyes squinted at the sun. "That old demon will buck her for sure and for certain."

"Who?" I asked him, wondering who could have the nerve to ride such a nervous and ornery horse.

"Zooie Marshall's girl. That Taffy. I told her it wasn't a fit horse to ride, but she got on it, anyway," Uncle Jack answered, shaking his head. "Knowed I never should of took that horse when that feller left it here. Said he'd be back for it and that was two year ago."

Taffy! My heart shouted and a huge lump jumped into my throat. Taffy on that old demon horse! The pinto was flying down the long slope of field heading into the woods. I shot a quick look at Uncle Jack. "Ain't you going to do something? Ain't you going to try to stop that old demon?"

"Nothing I can do, Lyon," Uncle Jack answered. "I ain't rid a horse in six or more years. Not with this bum leg I got. A bum leg won't let no man ride like he wants to."

I looked down at Uncle Jack's legs. Neither one ever seemed bum to me. But I didn't waste time thinking about that. All at once I was tearing out into the corral and making a flying leap onto Sagebrush, the only other horse Uncle Jack owned. Uncle Jack never tied up his horses; he just left them to roam and graze. Sagebrush reared back when I landed on him and whinnied, but he was as gentle as Scarlett or Rhett. When I kicked him in his flanks, he took off in a sudden gallop, out the open corral gate and across the field in the same direction Taffy and the old demon horse went.

"You're ridin' too fast without a saddle, Lyon!" Uncle Jack's voice was a part of the wind as I flew down the slope and charged for the woods.

I had a vision in my mind of Taffy laying somewhere deep in the woods with a broken neck, just laying there in agony and no one around to help her. The thought of it hit me so hard, I was near about to cry. Sagebrush swung into the woods and the first thing I saw when we flew past the overhanging branches of the trees and come into a small clearing was Taffy herself, still on the demon horse, looking as calm and collected as you please. The demon was standing still, his head lopped down, drinking water from the creek that ran through the woods. Taffy heard me and looked up just as I reined Sagebrush to a stop.

"What are you doing here, Lyon?" Taffy asked with a surprised look on her face.

I stared at her and swallered. There was something so beautiful about her sitting there on that old demon with her one long braid falling over her shoulder and her dark eyes flashing with devilment, that I almost couldn't speak.

"I . . . I thought . . . I thought that old hellion horse was going to throw you," I panted, all out of breath.

Taffy threw her head back and laughed a high, tinkling laugh that sounded like she thought I was a fool to worry about her. "You come after me because you love me, Lyon," she said, and her eyes flashed and glittered.

"I did not!" I practically choked on the words as I threw them out at her.

"You got too much caution in you, Lyon. You're too afraid to admit the truth."

"What do you know about the truth, Taffy?" I asked her with my eyes narrowed over her. Her face turned a deep red color then and her long dark eyelashes swooped down over her eyes for just a second, like she was ashamed to look at me. "How come you told your mama such a lie about me?" I went on.

Her eyes come up, full of fire. "To get me a doll for my collection," she answered, looking straight at me and not even blinking her eyes. "It's the Morocco doll with a little veil across its face. Oh, it's so precious!" It was so stupid, I couldn't believe it! I just sat there on Sagebrush staring at her like I was struck dumb. "Mama wouldn't and she wouldn't and she *wouldn't* believe me when I told her the truth, Lyon. But when I lied, she believed me."

"That's because she wanted to believe the very worst she could," I said bitterly. "You brought a lot of trouble on me, Taffy," I told her.

"I didn't want to, Lyon. Honest, I didn't want to." Tears sprang up in her eyes and she looked down.

The sun swept down through the lacy tree branches that stretched out above us and fell over Taffy. Her black hair suddenly flamed with red lights and the dress she was wearing, gray with little pink dots, seemed to turn all white in the sun's glare. Even the demon horse's hair turned a golden color with the sun in it. It was a picture. Like the paintings I'd seen over to Tylersville once when Aunt Ester took me to the place called an art gallery. They was all beautiful and filled with color that fair about dazzled the eyes. I never thought them paintings could be true to life until I saw Taffy in that moment with the sun shaking down through the leaves on her.

Taffy looked up and I'd never seen her eyes looking so deep and so hurt. "You believe me, don't you?" she asked, and her voice was all sweet and soft, like she'd never said a mean ner ornery thing in her life.

All of a sudden a chill run through me and my whole body seemed to shake with a strong emotion. It was peculiar to me and like I was lookin' at Taffy Marshall for the first time as a true girl. "Yes, I believe you," I said.

She reached up with her hand and tossed her braid over her shoulder, threw her head back, and laughed. Sagebrush moved beneath me, as startled at the sound as I was.

"You silly old fool boy!" Taffy cried, and all the sweetness was gone from her and she was the old Taffy again and, almost as fast as an eye can wink, she jabbed her heels into the demon and they was gone, flying out of the woods like wild, free birds, afraid of nothing.

I stared after them. There was no need to foller Taffy. I was sure she wouldn't be thrown by the horse. I couldn't hate her or even be too mad at her. The only person I could really be mad at was Zooie, for making Taffy into something wicked.

When I mentioned what happened at the supper table that night, Aunt Ester shook her head and said, "Zooie Marshall is raising that girl wrong. She'll be sorry someday."

"She's got a dirty mind, Zooie has," Uncle Clayborn said.

"Just remember this, son," Bear said to me. "A kiss is not bad. A kiss is wonderful and normal between a boy and a girl or a man and a woman, when it's what they both want."

"I wouldn't kiss that dirty Taffy's mouth even if it was made out of cherry pie!" I said disgustedly, and I took my hand and swiped it across my lips like I was taking away something sickening.

Bear reared back in his chair and laughed. "Geeehaaa! Someday you'll change your mind, boy. Maybe it won't be Taffy Marshall you'll be wanting to kiss, but it will be some girl."

"Trouble with Zooie," Uncle Clayborn went on, "she never could get over you falling in love with Theola and not her. She's always been a jealous woman."

I stared at Uncle Clayborn with my mouth open. Zooie jealous of my mama? Of Bear? I turned and stared at Bear.

"No need to bring that up," Aunt Ester said, and I stared at her.

Bear didn't even seem to pay no attention.

"Well, what do you say we go over and pay a visit to Miss Adeline tomorrow, Lyon? About time I took a gander at that miracle baby everyone is talking about, don't you think?"

I swallered so hard I was afraid everyone at the table would hear the food crash into my belly. I reckon I should of knowed Bear was always one to go on searching for the truth. I picked up my fork and started carving away at Aunt Ester's dumplings like I was trying to slice away tomorrow. When tomorrow come, it sure would be too soon for me.

10
Bear Starts Searching
for the Real Truth

The next day when me and Bear walked up on
Adeline's porch, she was standing at the door
looking out, just like as if she was expecting us.
The smile on her face was as bright as the
flowers in her yard.

"I heard you was back, Bear. I heard it and
I'm so glad. Come in. Come in, both of you. I
would of come over and greeted you, but I got
me a baby now and . . ." Adeline said, holding
the door open for us to go inside, and when she
mentioned the baby, her face lit up like she got
tangled up in the rays of the sun. ". . . and you
know how a little baby will confine a body to
the home," she went on.

"Talk is, you've got a 'miracle' baby, Adeline,"
Bear said, and I shot a gander at his face,
hoping I didn't look as guilty as I felt.

"And he's a pure beauty, Bear," Adeline said
with a proud smile. "He's all I ever wanted, and
more, too. Don't ever think the Lord don't

answer prayers, for he surely does."

I checked Bear's face again. There was a strong, doubtful look on it that made me wish I hadn't come with him. We follered Adeline into her little bedroom and looked down into the wood cradle that she had the baby laying in.

"My daddy made this cradle, Bear. He made it for his grandchildren to sleep in. That was over thirty years ago. He thought for sure me and Ferdie Hughs would be married. But Daddy died never seeing me and Ferdie marry ner having a grandchild of his own. Oh, how Daddy would love to know I got a little baby now, a little miracle baby, and that he's sleeping in the cradle he carved with his own two hands." Adeline sighed and reached into the cradle and gently moved the cover over the baby's shoulders.

"He's a right handsome little feller," Bear said softly. "How old is he, Adeline?"

"Well, I don't rightly know, Bear. But I reckon, according to Doc Gumble, he must be three months or more."

"How did he come to be on your front porch?" Bear asked after we'd quietly left the bedroom because the baby looked like we might be waking him up.

"Why, it was the Lord that placed him there. I thought you knew that," Adeline answered as she poured tea into cups and handed them to us. I couldn't stand Adeline's tea any better than I could stand Aunt Ester's, but I took it just to be polite.

"Adeline, I appreciate your faithfulness to the

Lord, but — " Bear started, and Adeline jumped right in.

"Now, Bear, don't you go and try to tell me that the Lord didn't put that little baby on my porch when I know blessed well he did! Don't you go and try to make me believe anything else. Because I won't! I won't because it just ain't true!"

Bear's eyebrows come together in a deep furrow and he looked at Adeline like he was worried about her. His eyes follered her into her kitchen, where she put cookies on a plate and brought them to us. He still stared at her while he nibbled on a cookie.

"I know why you're looking at me like that, Bear," Adeline said. "You're thinking in your mind that old Adeline's gone plumb addlepated. But it just ain't true. If you knew how I'd prayed for a little child to be with me . . ."

"What proof do you have that the Lord placed that baby on your porch?" Bear asked with the furrow still running down between his eyes.

"The baby is all the proof I need," Adeline replied firmly.

"Don't it seem strange to you that the Lord would lay a little baby out on your porch in a rainstorm . . ." Bear started, and Adeline dropped stiffly into a chair across the table from us. Bear leaned forward and changed his look to one of kindness. "Adeline, I'm not a cruel man to doubt the word of a good woman like you, but plain logical sense just don't match up with what you're telling me."

"The Lord works in mysterious ways, his wonders to perform, Bear," Adeline said.

"In my heart I'd like to believe it, but I got an itch inside me that says something's amiss, that somewhere there has to be someone who put that baby on your porch."

I gulped and started moving my foot around on the floor under the table, I was getting so nervous. I could even feel a sweat forming on my hands and under my arms. Bear reached for another cookie and turned it over and over, like he was studying it real hard.

Adeline pursed her lips up real tight and watched Bear closely. Bear just kept turning that old cookie over and over. Finally Adeline said, "I can tell you've been cogitating on this mighty strong, Bear. But you may as well forget — "

"What if that baby was stolen, Adeline? What if it was stolen from the mother?"

"Well, I never in all my born days!" Adeline cried.

Bear looked up from the cookie. "I was just thinking about the hunchback Gypsy."

The hunchback Gypsy! I froze! Was Bear thinking that the hunchback Gypsy had put the baby on Adeline's porch I wondered with my heart hammering like a train rumbling down the tracks. Everyone knew that the Gypsy sometimes stole things and could put a curse on you, if she was a mind to. And if she was a mind to, she'd take something off a person's property and leave something else in its place.

The Gypsy could do just about the meanest dang things you could think of, if she was a mind to.

"Have you missed anything around your yard?" Bear asked. "A chicken or a — "

"I won't listen, Bear Savage!" Adeline cried, and she jumped out of her chair and threw her hands over her ears and squeezed her eyes tightly closed.

Bear stood up and said sharply, "You *have* missed things."

Adeline opened her eyes and they was full of tears. She took down her hands and said in a pained voice, "Only an old laying hen, Bear. That's all. Just an old laying hen that wasn't worth a hoot ner a holler to me."

"What did the Gypsy leave? Tell me what she left in the hen's place, Adeline," Bear demanded.

"String! A ball of old rotten string! I'll show it to you. I threw it out, but I'll get it and . . ." Adeline cried.

"No," Bear said gently, "there's no need for that."

"It's the truth, Bear. The Gypsy left an old ball of dirty, rotten string that a clean person wouldn't even touch, much less use." Adeline's face was all crumpled up like she was going to go to crying. "You've got to believe me, Bear. Even the Gypsy wouldn't leave no live baby for an old hen! Where would the Gypsy get a little baby in the first place?"

"She'd steal it," Bear said. "Somewhere there could be a mother burning up inside over the loss of that little baby."

"No, Bear! This baby . . . *my* baby, is a gift from the Lord! The Lord put Miracle on my porch as sure as I'm standing here breathing and talking to you! It wasn't no hunchback, thieving Gypsy! It was the Lord!" Adeline sounded so desperate that I wanted to leap out of my chair and bound out of that house and run and run until I got rid of all the guilt inside me for what I'd done. But I knew the shadow of old J. Edgar Hoover, just and honest, would be dogging my steps all the way!

Bear took Adeline's hand in his and looked at her with kindness. "I wish I could believe that, Adeline."

"It's because you ain't right with the Lord, Bear," Adeline said, looking straight into Bear's eyes. But she said it in a soft voice, not like she was even angry. "If you was right with the Lord, you'd know he could do anything."

Bear sighed and looked down at Adeline's hand in his. "Adeline, I am right with the Lord in my own way. It's just, the feeling is in me so strong that there might be a mother out there who longs for her child."

A sadness come between Bear and Adeline then that I could see with my own eyes. It was like the whole room could feel it, and even the chair I was setting in. "Good day, Bear," Adeline said, and she pulled her hand out of Bear's hand.

Bear turned and looked at me and said, "Let's go, son. Let's go home now."

11
J. Edgar Hoover in Clement's Pond?

That night in bed, Bear said to me, "Well, at least Adeline don't think the stork brought that baby to her!" and he chuckled softly into a snore.

I wanted to tell Bear then. I wanted to. I really and truly did, but I just couldn't bring myself to. I'd get my mouth open and ready and, for some reason, it would snap closed. And once, when Bear was snoring real loud, I started to give his shoulder a little shake with my hand, but I couldn't make my hand move. Maybe I couldn't say anything because I really started wanting everyone to believe the Lord *had* put that little baby on Adeline's porch. Seemed like the whole town had changed since it got a miracle. Seemed like, in every store in town, you could go in and be greeted with a smile now instead of a snap and scowl. No sir, Clement's Pond never smiled so much ner looked so good ner felt so good, as far as I could tell.

In the days that follered, after me and Bear went to see Adeline, she was seen everywhere with that baby. She made a backpack out of canvas and strapped the baby into it and carried it on her back wherever she went. She was never without that little baby. Not for a minute.

"Leastways," everyone remarked, "she knows where that baby is all the time!"

It made my heart zing with happiness to see the change in Adeline. She had more bounce in her step, as she walked along the road with the baby strapped to her back, then ten of the youngest women in Clement's Pond, without a thing strapped to their backs. She had a big smile and greeting for everyone, and to know that I had a part in making her so happy brought a smile to my lips and a flutter to my heart when I saw her.

But I knew, in Bear's heart, that he believed somewhere there was a real mother of that little baby, and it seemed like I'd just be getting a lot of peace and contentment from thinking about Adeline with that baby when I'd think about Bear. Or there would be J. Edgar Hoover's name popping up on the radio or splashed across the front page of Uncle Clayborn's Tylersville newspaper, reminding me of what me and Justin and Sylvie had done. Then I'd take to *worrying* about Adeline being so happy.

"Bear," I said one afternoon as we laid on the grassy bank of the pond with our hickory fishing poles shoved down into the water, "do you think J. Edgar Hoover could ever come to Clement's Pond?"

"What for?" Bear asked. He had his eyes closed and his face was shaded by the oak-tree branches that hung over the edge of the pond.

"For . . . well, maybe to catch some criminal," I told him nervously.

"He might. But I doubt a man as big as he is in this country would take the time to come to a rock in the road like Clement's Pond. It would have to be a mighty big crime before he'd come here, I reckon."

I stared at Bear, halfway holding my breath. He was laying on his back with his arms behind his head, looking as peaceful as could be. Somewhere near the pond an old frog croaked out a tune and, close by, a couple of bumblebees zizzed at the daisies growing wild under the trees.

"How big?" I asked cautiously.

Bear opened his eyes and looked over at me and chuckled. "Very big," he said. "Why?"

"Why what?"

"Why are you asking about J. Edgar Hoover?"

"Oh . . . oh, I was just wondering, that's all."

"Well, I don't know of no big J. Edgar Hoover-type crime around here. Do you?" Bear sat up then and jiggled around with his fishing pole, but there wasn't no catch on it.

I jiggled around with mine just to look occupied. "No, sir," I said, throwing a quick look at Bear to see if he was looking at me.

"Don't look like we're going to catch any fish for your Aunt Ester to fry up for supper, do it, boy?" Bear said, standing up and pulling in his line.

"I reckon not," I said, and started pulling in my line.

"But my belly sure could use something in it right about now. How about yours?" Bear asked as he tossed his pole over his shoulder.

"Sure could," I said, and I stood up and pulled in my line and Bear said, "First I want to stop at Goad's store and see if I've got that letter I've been looking for."

"What letter, Bear?"

"From my partner. The one that wants me to go to Alaska."

It made my heart sink to hear Bear mention Alaska. All the way into town to Goad's store I held my breath, hoping that letter wouldn't be waiting. Every time I seen a clod in the road, I kicked it good and hard, trying to keep from pouring my heart out to Bear about how I didn't want him to go away again.

In Goad's store, Bear leaned over the counter and asked Mr. Goad about the letter. When Mr. Goad went to look, I studied the penny candy in a big jar on the counter. I reckoned Mr. Goad would offer me one. He always did. When he come back from looking for the letter, my eyes shot right to his hands. They was empty!

"Hadn't come in yet," Mr. Goad told Bear.

"You'll let me know when it does, won't you, George?"

"Sure will, Bear. Bring it out to you myself as soon as it comes in," Mr. Goad answered; then he looked at me. "Have a peppermint, Lyon?"

"No, thanks. Not this time," I told him.

Me and Bear walked around the store and

Bear picked out things to take home to Aunt Ester and all the while I was impatient to ask him what would be in the letter when it come. Bear paid for the purchases and we walked out of the store and I couldn't keep quiet any longer.

"What's it mean when you get the letter, Bear?"

"It'll mean that I should prepare to go to Alaska, son," Bear answered, and pulled out a hunk of cheese from the bag he carried and broke off a corner and handed it to me.

We started chewing together and headed down the road to Aunt Ester's. But all the time I had it in my mouth, I knew it was only there to keep me from talking. I knew Bear didn't want me to ask any more questions about him leaving.

12
In the Middle
of the Deep, Dark Woods

Soon as the letter come I knew Bear was going
to go away again. It was the end of spring and
the roads and fields was drying out from the
winter rains. The lupines and poppies and yeller
mustard grass was filling up the meadows and
the birds was coming back to sing in the trees.
Aunt Ester said we wouldn't need to have a fire
anymore, and she begun to sweep down the
cobwebs from the ceiling when old man Goad
come down the road, whistling and carrying a
long envelope in his hand. I was on the porch
scraping dried mud off my brogans when I
heard him whistling and I looked up. I saw the
letter and my whole heart flopped upside down
in my chest. Go back! Go back! I wanted to
shout to him, but I couldn't and he just kept
coming. When he reached the yard, he smiled
his big friendly smile and called out to me.

"Is your pa to home, Lyon? Got a letter here
for him."

Go back! I kept wishing I could yell, but my throat was all closed up and I couldn't even say a word. He come up on the porch and looked down at the letter in his hand. "Postmarked Alaska. Can you believe there's a place called 'Alaska,' Lyon? Must be a mighty cold place. I hear tell they've got people called Eskeemos living right in houses made out of ice. Now, can you beat that, Lyon? Where's your pa? Cat got your tongue? I reckon your pappy will be mighty glad to get this letter, the way he's been watching for it."

I reached up to take the letter, but the door popped open behind me and Aunt Ester grabbed for it and said, "Thanks a million, George, for bringing this letter out. I'll see Bear gets it. He ain't here right now. He's out in the woods with the old hunchback . . ."

Aunt Ester's words lodged in my brain like a nail being driven through! I didn't hear another word she said. ". . . He's out in the woods with the old hunchback . . ." rang in my ears like a loud gong.

I waited for Aunt Ester to close the door and for Mr. Goad to leave before I made a move. I could hear Aunt Ester singing inside the house as I pulled on my brogans. Then, glancing back at the kitchen winder, I hurried off the porch and down the road.

I didn't look back and I didn't stop running until I was at the woods' edge where two huge old oaks leaned toward each other and the heavy branches locked together overhead, closing off the sunlight. Entering the woods was like entering a dark cave. Way off in the distance, high up in the trees, I could hear birds chattering like they was mocking at me and telling me: "Go back, Lyon! You ain't got no business in these woods. Go back!" But I didn't go back and the birds just kept up a fuss. I hurried along and passed the clearing where I'd seen Taffy on the demon horse. I could hear the water making a soft swishing sound in the creek.

I kept going, walking deeper into the woods, until I come to the place where the old Gypsy's wagon was and stopped. The wagon didn't have any wheels on one side, and was propped up by two old oak-tree stumps. It leaned low on that side and looked like it might topple over at any minute. The Gypsy lived in it all alone and it was said that she ate live toads and lizards and anything else she could get her hands on. It made me plumb sick to think about all the things I'd heard tell the Gypsy could eat.

I snuck quiet as a cat along the side of the lopsided wagon. The paint on the wagon was peeling off and here and there I could see specks of the gaudy colors it used to be. Dirty gunnysacks hung at the winders for curtains and the strong smell of garlic whirled out at me as I passed and made my nose twitch and burn inside. I wondered if the Gypsy covered them lizards and frogs with garlic before she cooked them. There was a deep shadowed place surrounded by clumps of bushes and tangles of vines and decaying old trees just a little way from the wagon. I hadn't taken more than another step at the side of the wagon when I heard an angry, screeching sound and I knew it must be the hunchback Gypsy's voice. I stopped stone-still and listened.

"I ain't never took no chicken and I ain't never took nothing from no one! I'm not a thief!" It was the Gypsy all right, lying like that's all she knew how to do.

"You never took anything and never left anything in return for what you took?" It was Bear's voice, gruff and hard as nails.

"Well, now, that ain't stealin', is it? If you put something in something else's place — "

"Have you heard about the 'miracle' baby?" Bear cut right in and I thought sure I was going to gag and cough. Them old birds up in the trees sure was right. I didn't have no business here spying on Bear and the old Gypsy, but it looked like I couldn't of stopped myself if I'd tried.

"I heard tell, but I don't believe it," the Gypsy answered.

I edged as close to the end of the wagon as I could without being seen. I wanted to get a gander of Bear talking to the Gypsy, but when I finally got a gander at her, I wished I hadn't. When she come to town, she always wore a heavy dark coat and a thick covering over her head and she was so bent over that no one paid any attention to her face. This was the first true, up-close look I'd ever got of her. She had a wide, heavy brow and thick, dark skin and a long, sharp nose with gold in her teeth, and she was old and hunched over like she was sitting down, only she wasn't. She was standing at her true height and her head was twisted to the side as she stared up at Bear. And I could see the Gypsy had a strong and fierce eye, most likely so that she could see into the future and into what was past. A cold shiver run through me, just from looking at her.

"Can you tell me anything about that baby?" Bear asked, and I started shaking.

"I could make a potion, if I had a mind to."

I swallered and felt the pain of it all the way to my toes!

"What would it take to set your mind to it?" Bear asked, and I knew he was about ready to give the hunchback Gypsy anything she wanted, if it meant finding out where Adeline's baby come from.

"I'd need a lock of the baby's hair."

"What else?"

"A feather from a screech owl's back."

"Go on."

"A rabbit's foot from a fresh-killed rabbit."

"Anything else?"

"Food. For me. Enough to keep me for a while. Some pork and beef and fixings to set close to my bones."

"When should I have everything?" Bear asked.

"Bring it all at the first full moon. If you wait a day, don't come. The potion will only work on the first night of the full moon."

"You'll have it, Gypsy," Bear said, and he turned quickly and stalked away into the thick brush.

I didn't wait to see what the Gypsy would do next. I was too busy hightailing it away from there. I ran so fast I thought my feet would fall off, but they didn't, and I kept going. I made it to the two oak trees and stopped to catch my wind; then I hurried on, afraid I'd meet Bear on the way home. I didn't, though. Somehow I got home and beat it into the house and finished washing up for supper before Bear's big boots come clumping across the front porch. Soon as he walked through the door, Aunt Ester headed to get the letter, saying, "Oh, Bear, there's a letter come for you today. George Goad brought it over."

I watched Bear's face as he stood reading the letter, then folded it and stuck it down in his shirt pocked.

"What do it say, Bear?" Uncle Clayborn asked as he shook the ashes out of his pipe into a tin can beside his chair.

"It's from my partner. Says the weather's fine and I ought to set about leaving for Seward. He's got a cabin and supplies and six wild horses just ripe for the breaking," Bear answered.

"Oh, Bear. I was in hopes you'd change your mind and stay to the end of summer and be with the boy more, do all the things he's been looking to do with you," Aunt Ester said from the kitchen doorway, wiping her hands on her apron.

I was standing beside Uncle Clayborn's chair when Bear looked at me and said, "Lyon understands, don't you, son?"

I felt my chin begin to quiver and my eyes fill up with tears. I knew if I stayed there a minute more, I'd bust out bawling and I wouldn't be able to stop. All at once I spun around and charged for my bedroom.

"Lyon!" Bear shouted.

"The boy's got a heavy heart, Bear. A real heavy heart about you going away. You ought not to leave him again," Aunt Ester said, and I could hear her as clear as if the walls was made out of bed sheets.

The slow, heavy thump of Bear's boots headed toward the bedroom and just as I shoved my face into my quilt to smother my sobs, he opened the door. He come to the bed and set down on it and touched my shoulder with a gentle hand. He sat quiet for a long time with his hand still on my shoulder, and when I stopped crying, he said softly, "I'll be back, son. Didn't I make a commitment to you?"

I lifted my head and stared through my swollen eyes at Bear. "Don't mean nothing!" I said in a thick, raw voice. "You'll come back when you get good and ready! But, why do you go? Why can't you be like other daddies? Why do you have to be so danged *different?*"

"Because I *am* different, son," Bear said gently.

"Well, I don't like you being different! I hate you being different!" I yelled. "I hate you and I hate you always being different!"

Soon as I said it, I wished I hadn't. I bit down hard on my lip and prayed I could take back all them mean words, but the Lord wasn't about to let me. Bear stared at me for a second with a deep hurt look on his face; then he pulled me into his arms and held me so tight and so hard, I thought my ribs would crack in two.

After a while, he moved back and looked down at me. "I have to be me, Lyon. I can't be no one else. If you love me as your daddy, then you have to accept me just as I am."

"I . . . love you, D-Daddy," I told him in a trembling voice.

"I know you do, son. But you got to accept me, too," Bear said. "And you got to believe me when I say I'll be back sooner this time."

"Yes, sir," I said. And that night I told my mama all about what went on between me and Bear. She didn't say nothing, though. She just smiled her angel smile out of the picture at me.

The next morning as I was dressing for school, I heard Uncle Clayborn say, "Bear's got him a strong wanderlust, for sure and for certain."

Aunt Ester sighed heavily and said, "It's a hard cross to carry, Clayborn, loving a dead wife all these years, and looking for her in every face he sees and running away from hisself, knowing he'll never find her. The dead are very, very dead, indeed." She sighed again, and just as I walked into the kitchen, I heard Uncle Clayborn whisper, "Shush! The boy . . ."

Times like them, I wished the walls of the house was as thick as the vaults in the bank over to Tylersville, where they keep all that money. I'd of give just about anything if I didn't have to hear such talk!

"Well, Lyon, good morning," Aunt Ester said brightly, like as if she hadn't said a word or sighed a sigh.

"Better get a move on, boy," Uncle Clayborn said.

Just before I left for school I asked, "When is the next full moon, Aunt Ester?" By then Uncle Clayborn had already gone out the barn to slop the hogs.

"The next full moon? Hummm ... I'll have to look on the calendar. Why do you want to know?"

"I was just wondering, that's all."

"Well, while you're wondering, you'd better wonder on out to the bus stop," Aunt Ester said.

At the bus stop I saw Taffy and Sylvie with their heads together and Justin jabbing the toes of his boots into the ground. I went up to him and all at once Sylvie shouted out, "Justin's got the lice! He caught them from T-Roy Tate!"

"Liar!" Justin yelled in a fury.

Sylvie and Taffy started giggling and falling all over each other. The bus come and we got on. Sylvie and Taffy plopped down in the seat behind me and Justin, and we could hear them giggling as the bus started off, saying silly things about Justin having the lice and all. When we got a fur piece down the road, Sylvie popped her head over the back of our seat and whispered close to my ear, "I seen Miles Standish yesterday. Old Adeline was coming out of Viola's hat shop carrying him on her back like a papoose. Well, it won't be long and that

little baby will be all mine and Adeline Newberry can go stick her skinny neck straight
down in the pond!"

I looked up at her. "What are you saying,
Sylvie?" I hissed.

Sylvie squinted her eyes and mashed her lips
together till she looked plumb ugly and evil.
Then she said like an old devil, "You'll see," and
plopped back into her seat.

I leaned close to Justin. "I don't like the way
Sylvie is talking."

"Aw, don't worry. She don't mean half what
she says."

I leaned even closer, so close I could smell the
breakfast bacon on Justin's breath. "Bear went
into the woods and saw the hunchback Gypsy..."
Justin's eyes grew wide. "He's trying to find out
who put the baby on Adeline's porch. He don't
believe for one minute the Lord done it. He
thinks the Gypsy can tell him..."

"Holy jumpin' earwigs!" Justin said, and
scooted down in the seat.

All the rest of the way to school I thought
about the hunchback Gypsy and wondered how
Bear would get the lock of hair from Miracle
and all the other things the Gypsy wanted to
make a potion. If anyone could find out something deep and dark and secret, it was the
Gypsy, I thought with a shudder. And I thought
about J. Edgar Hoover coming to Clement's
Pond looking for "the person or persons who
stole away in the night after leaving a baby on
Adeline Newberry's porch." I could hear it on

the radio already and see Aunt Ester and Uncle Clayborn all hunched over with their ears pressed up close, listening to J. Edgar Hoover hisself making a plea to all good citizens to report anything they know to the FBI. It was a miserable day. One of the worst I could remember, except for all the days that Bear went away from Clement's Pond.

13
A Feather, Rabbit's Foot and Lock of Hair

One morning a week later, Bear got up bright and early and left the house. He come back with a rabbit's foot and the feather out of an old screech owl's back. I didn't ask him how he got them and he didn't show them to me. He had them poked into a canvas satchel and hung in the closet, back out of the way, so no one could see it. It didn't take long for me to find the satchel, and when I did, I wasn't surprised to hear Bear mention to Aunt Ester that it looked like Adeline's baby needed a hair trim. I didn't have to look at the calendar to know the full moon had come, neither.

"Where do you get your brains, Bear?" Aunt Ester asked, giving Bear a curious, puzzled look. "Little babies don't need their hair cut."

"This baby does," Bear said firmly.

"Oh, flitter!" Aunt Ester exclaimed, shaking her head and pursing her lips up tight.

Since it was Saturday, I put up a fuss to go to

Adeline's with Bear. Finally Bear said, "Well, I reckon you can go, boy. I don't see why not." But there wasn't any eagerness in his voice to have me go with him.

"I swear to goodness, Bear, every time you go away, you come back a little more addlepated than when you left!" Aunt Ester said as me and Bear took off out of the house.

We lit off down the road with Aunt Ester watching us from the kitchen winder. In just a few minutes we were at Adeline's house and Bear didn't waste no time in telling her what he wanted.

"Adeline," he said, "I'd feel right proud if you'd let me have a little lock of Miracle's hair . . . to carry just for luck, you understand."

"Why, Bear, what a lovely request. I'm sure the Lord would be pleased for you to have it. A lock of hair from a miracle baby is sure to bring you all kinds of good luck," Adeline said happily, and she hurried out of the bedroom to get a pair of scissors from her sewing basket. She was back in no time and handing Bear the scissors. Bear reached down into the cradle and quickly snipped off a little twig of hair from the front of Miracle's head.

"Now look at you," Bear said, smiling down at Miracle. "As happy a little critter as I've ever seen."

Miracle kicked his legs and gurgled and cooed. Looked like he'd got chubby since Adeline had been taking care of him. His cheeks was as round as little balls. "Yes, he is a happy and sweet baby," Adeline said, giving Miracle a tender look. "The Lord hasn't told me how old he is yet, but He will by and by."

"How do you know, Miss Adeline?" I asked.

"Because I know He will. Everything will be revealed in due time," she answered me.

I swallered and studied Adeline's face carefully, wondering if she was predicting the future without even knowing it. She looked back down at Miracle and I squeezed my eyes shut, wishing all that had happened would blow away and get lost in the wind. When I opened my eyes, Bear had his finger stuck in Miracle's hand and was swinging it gently back and forth.

"You've got quite a grip there, little feller," Bear said, and Miracle smiled. "You'll make a good strong farmer one of these days."

"Not that boy! Not my Miracle!" Adeline said with an emphatic smack of her lips. "That boy's going to get his schooling and be a doctor or a lawyer . . ."

"You've got his future all planned out, ain't you, Adeline?" Bear said, and there was a sadness in his voice that Adeline didn't seem to hear.

"That I have, Bear," she said softly, and she gazed down into the cradle with a loving smile on her face.

Bear pulled his finger out of the baby's grip. "No one could raise a child any better than you, Adeline," he said in a soft, kindly way. Then to me he said, "We'd best be going, son." There was a sad look on his face and in his eyes and I knew for a fact that he didn't and never would believe that little baby was a pure miracle.

"So soon? I've got oatmeal cookies..."

"I just stopped by to tell you good-bye, Adeline. In case I don't get to see you before I leave," Bear told her.

"Seems like you're always going away, Bear," Adeline said, and she looked down at me and touched my cheek with her warm hand. I already felt so bad. Looking at Adeline and knowing she felt sorry for me because of Bear's going away again would only make me feel a hundred times worse. We went out on the front porch and Adeline said, "Maybe someday you'll come home to stay."

Bear smiled at me and put his hand on my head. "I'm thinking on doing just that, Adeline."

We started down the steps and Adeline come to the edge of the porch and said with a serious sound in her voice, "Bear, that last time you was here, we had a hard word between us..."

Bear stopped and looked back at her. "No such of a thing," he said.

"Now, Bear, you know we did and I want to apologize to you for saying you wasn't right with the Lord. I'm plumb ashamed I said it."

Bear walked back up the steps and hugged Adeline. "You get shut of your worrying about things that don't matter, Adeline."

When we left Adeline's and started down the road, I asked Bear where we was going next. He was mighty secretive and quiet for a minute. Then he said, "You're going back home to do your chores before it gets dark and I'm going rambling for a spell." I could tell Bear had the hunchback Gypsy on his mind.

After supper I pretended I was so sleepy I couldn't hardly hold my head up and Aunt Ester told me to go on to bed, that I needed my rest, it looked like. Only I didn't go to bed. I sat at my winder and waited for darkness to fall and the moon to come up bright and clear. Soon as it did, and I heard Aunt Ester and Uncle Clayborn occupied with getting ready for bed, I threw my leg over the sill and got out that winder and ran around the house to the road as fast as I could. I ran until I got to Justin's house and went to his bedroom winder and peered inside.

I didn't see Justin anywhere in the room so I hurried around to the kitchen and looked inside. There he was, at the table, doing his homework, it looked like. I picked up an acorn from the ground and tossed it against the glass. Justin's head snapped toward the winder. I tossed another acorn and he jumped up and come to the winder and peered out.

"It's me! Lyon!" I called, but I did it in a low voice so no one in the house would hear me.

Justin come out the back door looking surprised. "What are you doing here, Lyon?" he asked.

"Bear has gone into the woods to see the old Gypsy. She's going to build up a potion and ask it questions."

"Holy jumpin' earwigs!" Justin exclaimed. "You reckon Bear is going to ask about the baby?"

"For sure and for certain," I said. "That's why we've got to go, to find out what answers the Gypsy gives Bear."

"My daddy would tar and feather me if he knew I went into the woods at night, but that's a chance I'll just have to take," Justin said, glancing around at the house. "Everyone will be going to bed soon. Wait here."

"Hurry!" I told him, and I went to lean against the house in the darkness, out of the light of the moon, in case someone stepped out the door besides Justin. After I was there awhile, I heard Sylvie yell out, "What you going to bed so early for?" And Justin come back with "Mind your own snoopy business!" Then Mrs. Bogart hollered, "You two young'uns hush!" I wished Justin would hurry. The moon seemed to be getting bigger and fatter, and it shined its light right into my face, making a shadow of me on the wall of the house. I heard a noise, leaves crumpling on the ground, and at the edge of my eye I saw a dark figure appear from the side of the house, moving closer.

"Let's go," Justin said, stepping into the moonlight.

I breathed a sigh of relief and we took off like Oscar Bebee's bull was after us and got to the place where the oak trees arched together at the opening of the woods, just as the moon was beginning to throw out its strongest light. We was out of breath and stopped only for a minute to catch our wind. Then we took off again, hurrying through the woods to the deepest part, where the Gypsy lived. When we got close to the old lopsided wagon we could hear the sound of voices. We crept alongside the wagon, trying to be as quiet as the lizards that skittered around under the pine needles, and peered around the end of the wagon. What we saw made us catch our breath! The Gypsy was standing close to an old black-looking washtub that was set up on a kindling-wood fire. In her hand was what looked like a broomstick and she was stirring it round and round, looking into the washtub like she couldn't take her eyes away. Bear was close by, watching her with a hard frown on his face.

"See, I told you that old Gypsy was a witch!" Justin hissed. "What's she stirring?"

"That's her potion," I whispered back. "She's got the screech owl's feather and the rabbit's foot and the lock of Miracle's hair that Bear brought her in that old washtub."

"Holy pinchin' earwigs! It smells like puke!" Justin said, making a sour face.

"Quiet!" I warned him.

"How long before you have an answer? Tell me, Gypsy," Bear said.

"When the potion bubbles for ten minutes without stop, you'll have the answer to your questions, Bear Savage," the Gypsy answered.

"Why ten minutes?"

"The skin on the rabbit's foot has to boil off and mix with the feather and the baby's hair. It has to boil and bubble good. The bigger the bubbles, the more the potion tells," the Gypsy answered, still stirring the awful brew.

I was so nervous about what that potion was going to tell that I was near about to fainting dead away. Seemed like every nerve in my body was trembling. I looked around and checked

Justin's face. He looked like he was feeling the same way.

"Do you think the Gypsy will really get the truth out of that old nasty-smelling pot?" Justin whispered, and his voice was shaking.

"I don't know," I whispered back, and my voice was shaking too.

"What if it tells what we done — ?"

"Shooo!" I hissed, and looked back at Bear and the Gypsy.

"It's beginning to bubble," the Gypsy said, and her eyes got bigger and bigger as she stirred the foul-smelling stuff.

I could see the tension building up on Bear's face. His jaw looked tight enough to spring apart and his eyes was hard set and filled with moonlight as he watched the potion. The red flames licked shadows across his face as they climbed up the sides of the washtub. The light from the moon was so bright it looked like daylight had come. I swallered again and again, wondering what the Gypsy would find in the potion.

"Do you reckon that potion can tell names?" Justin asked, and his voice was near about strangled.

"I don't know . . ."

The Gypsy stopped stirring the brew and looked up at Bear. The firelight was in her black eyes and on her face and it made her look meaner and uglier than I'd ever thought anyone could look.

"Well?" Bear asked, scowling impatiently at

the Gypsy. "What is it? Tell me, hunchback!"

"It ain't a perfect boil. I can't tell you at this time," the Gypsy answered, and Bear looked about ready to explode.

"Why? Why can't you tell me? You have the feather and the baby's hair and the rabbit's foot!" Bear roared like he really was a bear.

"I can only tell you that the baby was left on the old maid's porch by human hands," the Gypsy answered, narrowing her eyes over Bear.

"*Whose* human hands?" Bear demanded, looking violent.

"More than one person's. That is all I can say at this time."

"*More* than one? You mean *two? Two* people?" Bear roared again.

"Or three . . ."

"*Three?*" The firelight danced over Bear's face like angry hands. He looked fit to be tied. "Who were they? Give me names."

"It is all I can tell you, Bear Savage!" the Gypsy cried with her eyes flashing. "To know more than this, you'd have to come at the next full moon — "

"I won't be here!" Bear exploded. "I'll be far gone to Alaska! I have to know now. Before I leave. I can't go away with this question in my mind!" I'd never seen Bear looking so much like old-billy-hell had broke loose in him.

The Gypsy dropped the broomstick and moved away from the washtub. "Three people. That is *all* I can tell you, Bear Savage!" she screeched.

Justin and me exchanged a frozen look of fear. Nothing inside us was frozen, though. We was wobbling and shaking like a three-legged table.

Bear sighed and shoved his hands down into his pockets and stared into the washtub. "I wish I could see what you see, Gypsy," he said, and suddenly the Gypsy raised her head and cackled in a strange, loud voice. So loud and so strange that Justin started to bolt and run.

I grabbed his arm, but he pulled and tugged and lurched away from me. It scared me so much that I took off in a wild run right behind him. We ran, streaking through the scrubby woods, follering the trail of moonlight until we reached the two arching trees and collapsed against them.

"She . . . she . . . the o-old G-Gypsy knew, Lyon! S-she knew!" Justin panted, and there was horror in his face.

We could hear twigs snapping and pine needles being scuffed through behind us. Bear! Bear walking quickly through the woods! We tore away from the trees and ran until we gagged for breath, until we almost fell to the ground, until our legs, flying over the under-brush and ruts in the road, felt like propellers moving up on. Finally we reached Justin's yard and fell on the cool, damp pine needles and grass, breathing like as if our lungs would split open. I pressed my face into the stiff pine needles and soft blades of grass and lay there until all the faintness and dizziness in my body fled away. It seemed like forever before I was able to breathe like myself and could raise up and look at Justin. He was laying flat on his belly with his arms and legs spread out. He looked as dead as a doornail.

"Justin . . ." I whispered. "Justin, are you alive?"

His arms and legs twitched and he moved a little. "Nope . . ." he answered in a muffled voice.

"I ain't neither," I told him. "Leastways, if I don't get home and inside the house before Bear does, I'll wish I was dead!"

14
Undoing a True Love Vow

The morning Bear left, I walked down to the train depot with him and he told me all he thought I ought to know about what he was going to do in Alaska. "You ever heard of felling timber, boy?" he asked me.

"Yes, sir," I spoke up.

"Well, that's what I'm going to do when I get to Alaska. Going to clear some land and build some cabins and corrals and bring in some horses and start up a ranch."

"What kind of trees they got in Alaska, Bear?"

"Spruce and birch and hemlock and cedar and evergreen and you name it," he answered, swinging his satchel to his other shoulder and smiling down at me. Seemed like Bear never looked so good. His eyes was all asparkle and his beard was brushed right into perfection. He had on his tan suede breeches and vest and the brown broadcloth shirt Aunt Ester made him and boots that went almost to his knees. I was mighty proud of Bear, for sure and for certain.

"What you going to do with all that timber after you build the cabin and corrals and things?" I asked him.

"Sell it to the paper mills, I reckon."

"Why do you want to start up a ranch, Bear?"

"It ain't so much for me as it is for my partner. He's got the biggest itch. All I'm going to do is scratch it for a while."

"Does that mean you're going to keep your promise?" I asked anxiously.

Bear stopped walking and looked down at me. "Ain't that what I told you, Lyon? A promise is a promise." He reached out and rested his hand on my head. "I'll be back before winter sets in good and heavy."

Bear was going to take the train as far as Tylersville; then he was going to hitch rides however he could until he got across the country. Then he'd just go on to Alaska the best way he knew how. Bear knew a lot about roughing it. He never let anything get in the way of his movement. After he got on the train, he stood out on the caboose with his satchel tossed over his shoulder and the bag of food Aunt Ester give him tucked under his arm. The train give a quick jolt and started moving and I ran along the tracks, trying to keep up.

"You mind your Aunt Ester and Uncle Clayborn!" Bear yelled out.

"Yes, sir!" I yelled back over the clatter of the train rolling along the tracks.

"And say your prayers at night and remember your mama in them!"

"Yes, sir!" I panted, and all at once the train picked up speed and before I knew it, Bear was disappearing, getting farther and farther away from me. It seemed, after a while, he wasn't nothing but a tiny speck standing on the caboose and waving when his wild "Geeeehaaaaa!" broke loose and exploded across the valley. Tears come into my eyes then and I shoved my hands down into my pockets and took off in a run for home, past all the people standing around the depot, down the main road of town. Everything was just a blur in my eyes.

When I reached home, Aunt Ester was washing up all the dishes from the big dinner she'd cooked before Bear left. "You're going to be lonesome for a while," she said right off. "That's only natural. But you'll soon get used to Bear being gone again. You always do."

"I won't never get used to Bear being gone!" I told her, trying not to cry.

Aunt Ester stopped what she was doing and stared at me with a frown of kindness on her face. "Go ahead on and have your cry, boy," she said gently. "You don't have to hold back because of me."

I looked away from her and swiped at the tears that started down my cheeks. Then I ran into Aunt Ester's arms and buried my face in her big gathered apron that smelled like fried-chicken grease and white-flour-gravy drippings and cried. Bear going away was like the whole world and everything in it dying and leaving me all alone.

It looked like it wasn't enough that I was grieved over Bear going away and the hunchback Gypsy knowing about the baby. I guess that wasn't enough to have to worry about. Seemed like Sylvie *just had* to come along and make things worse for me. A week or two later, when Aunt Ester's marigolds and four-o'clocks was coming up good all around the house and dandelions was showing up everywhere, Sylvie come to the house and asked me to sit out on the front-porch steps with her. I didn't want to, but I reckoned I'd better, just to appease her.

"You two better not go to spooning!" Uncle Clayborn chuckled, and Aunt Ester snapped, "Clayborn Tarver, you mind what you say!"

Me and Sylvie set down on the bottom step of the porch and she spread the skirt of her dress out on her legs all prim and proper and looked at me. I'd of give anything to jump up and run in the house!

"Lyon, me and you ain't been together much lately. Seems to me you might of forgot all about our true-love vow."

I looked down at the ground. "I ain't forgot," I told her miserably.

"You swore you'd love me till the day you die, Lyon. Our own blood run together to seal our vow. You got my blood and I got yours. Lyon, look up and face me!"

I swallered hard and looked up. "It would pain my whole insides out if you was thinking about other girls," Sylvie said, with her blue eyes flashing over me.

"I ain't thinking of no other girl, Sylvie," I told her. And I wasn't right then.

Sylvie smiled like as if I'd just told her all I ever did was lay around and moon over her. She stretched her skirt tight over her knees and leaned close to me. "Lyon, don't you know it's near about killed me seeing Adeline Newberry with little Miles Standish, walking all over town like as if *she* found that baby and not me! I been thinking of just going right up to her and telling her to give me that baby!"

"You can't do that!" I exploded, and I looked up at the house, hoping Aunt Ester and Uncle Clayborn hadn't heard me. I lowered my voice. "No telling what would happen to Adeline if that little baby was took from her."

"Don't you think Adeline would survive? Anyone that lived in the world all alone as long as she would survive! What does an old maid need with a baby, anyway? She ain't got no man to be a father to it!"

"And neither have you!"

"But I will someday. Me and you made a true-love vow, Lyon. That means, more than likely, we'll be getting married. I already told Mama what kind of dress I want and everything."

I near about swallered my tongue! I couldn't believe what I was hearing! Somehow I got myself organized so I could speak. "Sylvie, I swear to you, on this day, if you take that baby away from Adeline, I'll never speak to you again as long as I live!" I started to tremble after I'd said it, thinking I might jump up and push Sylvie plumb off the step.

Sylvie stood up and I could see the fire spitting in her eyes. "Don't tell me that, Lyon. We made a true-love vow and it can't be broke. I got your blood . . ." A quiver rose up in her voice and I looked down again because I didn't want to see her go to crying and start feeling sorry for her. I wanted to hate her because of her wanting to take Miracle away from Adeline and because she knowed what it would do to Adeline and didn't care. I didn't know how I could of made a true-love vow with a girl so evil.

"I don't care! I don't care if you have got my blood!" I shouted in a fury, and Aunt Ester come rushing to the door and shoved it open and just as she did, Sylvie took off in a run across the yard and down the road yelling back, "You'll be sorry, Lyon! You just wait and see!"

Aunt Ester stepped out on the porch and said, "What's going on out here, Lyon?"

I looked up at her. "Nothing, Aunt Ester," I said, and I wondered if my tongue was filling up with lying warts.

The next day, all I knew was, I wanted to undo that true-love vow I'd made with Sylvie. I wanted to take back every word I could remember saying. I didn't love Sylvie Bogart and I didn't want no love vows floating around. I couldn't take back the blood that run with hers when she pricked our palms with Aunt Ester's sewing needle, but I reckoned it didn't flow down too far under the skin, anyway. I wished there was someone I could ask about how to take the vow back. I couldn't think of no authority on love living in Clement's Pond, so I decided the next best thing was to go talk to Uncle Jack. He had been married twice that I'd heard tell of. Nobody knew where his used-to-be wives was, but I figured any man who had two wives ought to know all about how to break a vow.

When I went up on Uncle Jack's front porch, I could hear him inside the house puttering around, talking to his cats. I knew he must be feeding them because I could hear the cats meowing and fussing like everything. I opened the door and went inside and headed for the kitchen. Sure enough, Uncle Jack was pouring food out of a plate onto the floor and all them cats was slithering over his feet and climbing up his pant legs and falling all over each other, trying to get to that food.

"Selfish critters!" Uncle Jack exploded at the cats. "You'll get yourn! Don't be so blamed selfish, Elmira!" He lifted his leg and flipped Elmira off his shoe.

"Hello, Uncle Jack," I said from the doorway.

He looked up, then back down at all the cats as they scurried around trying to get to the food on the floor. "How you be there, Lyon?" he said. "Did you ever see such selfish critters in all your born days? Get some cream out of the box over yonder and pour some in them bowls on the floor, will you?"

"Sure thing, Uncle Jack," I said, and I hurried to do what Uncle Jack told me. Soon as I started pouring the cream into them bowls, half the cats scampered away from Uncle Jack and skittered across the floor where I was. They started lapping at the cream before it even touched the bowl. I had to jump away and start pouring the cream in another bowl just to get away from them starved cats.

"Look at them durned cats, Lyon. Wild as heatherns, ain't they? No concern a'tall for the next feller. Just like the human species," Uncle Jack said, and raked more food out of the plate onto the floor.

"Yes, sir," I said and I filled up all the bowls halfway and the jar was empty.

"Just put that jar in the sink there, Lyon," Uncle Jack told me.

I did what he said and follered him out on the front porch and watched him while he picked up papers and tossed them into other spots. I thought it was funny how Uncle Jack was always willing to bend down and move things out of the way, but seemed like he never got around to picking anything up permanent. After he moved a few papers around, he headed for the ladder that leaned up against the side of the house. I follered him.

"I'll have this roof fixed in no time," Uncle Jack said as he started up the ladder.

"Uncle Jack," I said quickly. I had to ask before he got up on the roof. "Uncle Jack, the reason I come over is . . ."

Uncle Jack stopped middle way of the ladder and looked down at me. All at once I felt embarrassed and had to look down at the ground.

"You come over for what, Lyon?"

I looked up at him again, wishing I knew how

to say it good, but I didn't, so I just had to say it the way it fell out of my mouth. "Uncle Jack, I come to ask you if you know how a person can break a true-love vow." I swallered after I said it and looked down at the ground again. I could hear Uncle Jack moving back down the ladder. When I looked up again, he was leaning against the ladder and staring hard at me.

"A true-love vow, you say?"

"Yes, sir. I've got to know."

Uncle Jack rubbed his chin and studied the ground. "Well, now . . . it depends on whether or not it's a legal love vow or just a simple spoken love vow. If it's a legal one, like marriage . . ."

"Oh, no, sir. It ain't," I said real quick.

"Well, then it depends who it's with."

"It's with a girl. Er . . . some girl this feller I know give a true-love vow to and now he wishes he didn't and he wants to break it." My breath was coming pretty fast after a lie like that.

"Well, alls this feller's got to do is go to the girl and tell her he ain't interested no more and walk away."

"It ain't that easy. See, Syl . . . I mean, *this girl*, she's odd. She would have a flat-out duck-down fit if I . . . I mean, if *this feller* I know did it that way."

"How else can you . . . I mean, *he* do it, Lyon? If you . . . I mean, *he* wants to break a vow he made to Syl . . . I mean, to a *girl*, alls you . . . I mean, *he* can do is tell her and turn and make dust."

I frowned and looked down at the ground again. Walking away from Sylvie would be like inviting a tornado to swoop down over me and lay me out flatter than a flitter! Uncle Jack started up the ladder. I looked up and watched him reach the roof and step off the ladder onto it.

"Tell your friend that vows was meant to be broken!" he yelled down at me with a loud chuckle.

What Uncle Jack told me just didn't satisfy me. It didn't seem right to break a vow and go on off. It seemed like a person ought to say something soothing first. Especially to a girl like Sylvie. Trouble was, I didn't know no soothing words to say. I left Uncle Jack's place and started walking home with my head bent down and kicking at all the dirt clods along the road. Just as I kicked one old clod and it scattered into dust, someone called out to me.

"Good afternoon, Lyon."

I looked up. Adeline Newberry was in her yard picking roses out of the bushes growing along the fence.

"Hello, Miss Adeline," I said. It made me plumb sick to look at her and know what Sylvie had in mind of doing.

"What do you hear from your father?"

"I ain't hardly had time to hear from him yet," I told her.

"Oh, of course you haven't. Bless me, I never do mark time the way most folks do."

Suddenly I had an idea. I stopped walking and went up to the fence just as Adeline turned to go up to her porch. I stood at the fence and watched her sit down on the steps and poke a rose up into her hair. The baby was laying in a basket on the porch and Adeline reached out and give it a little touch and a smile.

"Miss Adeline?" I called, and she turned back and looked at me.

"Yes, Lyon?"

"Miss Adeline . . ."

"Come through the gate, Lyon."

I opened the gate and went inside the yard.

"Come sit up here with me and Miracle."

I went over and sat down on the step and lifted my head up so I could see in the basket. Miracle rolled his big blue eyes all around and jabbed his fists in the air and kicked his legs in all directions. He went to gurgling and gooing so much, spit drooled all down his chin. I felt plumb sorry for that baby, knowing all I knowed about him.

"Miss Adeline," I said, looking at her. "I been meaning to come by and ask you how the baby is doing."

"He's doing just fine, thank you, Lyon. As you can see, he's growing and happy." Adeline smiled and I could feel a heavy pull in my heart. She sure loved that baby. Anyone could see that.

"Miss Adeline, I also been meaning to ask you a question," I said, and cleared my throat.

"Yes, Lyon? Go on."

I cleared my throat again. "Well, it's about true-love vows . . ."

She looked mighty thoughtful for a minute. Like she was thinking the matter over right smart. Finally she said, "True-love vows? What do you want to know about true-love vows, Lyon?"

I had to clear my throat again. "Well, what I want to know is, how would a person go about breaking one?"

"Oh my, Lyon. A person should never break a vow. Especially not a true-love vow. A vow is a promise. A promise is your sacred word. Breaking a true-love vow would be the same as breaking a heart."

That, for sure and for certain, wasn't what I wanted to hear. I stood up. "Well, I have to go now . . ."

"Wouldn't you like a nice piece of my raisin pie? It's just fresh out of the oven."

"No, thank you, Miss Adeline," I told her, and I jumped up and whipped through the yard, slamming the gate behind me. I knew Adeline's eyes was on me as far as she could see me running down the road.

When I got home Uncle Clayborn opened his eyes and stared at me from the divan where he was laying. "Simmer down, boy! No need to run in here like your britches was on fire," he said with a yawn, and closed his eyes again.

Out in the kitchen I could hear Aunt Ester singing loudly: "Lorrrrrd and Saaaaavior, truuuuue and kiiind . . . be the maaaaster of my miiind . . ."

When I got in the kitchen she was at the sink scrubbing out a big pot. "Aunt Ester," I said, and I was as nervous as one of Uncle Jack's old cats, to ask her. Her back was to me and she looked tall and strong in a flowered dress and the wide bow of a white apron tied at her waist. She didn't hear me and she kept up her singing with her long, thick arms moving up and down as she scrubbed the pot.

"Bleeesss and streeenthhhhen all my powerrrs of thooought and willl . . ."

"Aunt Ester," I said again, louder.

Aunt Ester looked around then and saw me and asked, What's on your mind, boy?"

I went up to her and leaned against the sink. "Aunt Ester, I've got to know something."

"Is it about school and book learning?"

"No, ma'am, it ain't about nothing like that."

"Is it about not wanting to do your chores? Because if it is —"

"No, ma'am."

"Then speak up, boy." She went back to pouring the elbow grease on that pot and started humming at her song.

"Aunt Ester, there's this feller I know, who shall remain nameless, who made a true-love vow with someone . . . a girl, I mean."

Aunt Ester stopped humming and looked at me and chuckled. "How old is this feller who shall remain nameless?"

"What difference does that make?"

"Because, boy, nobody under the age of twenty-one should be held responsible for a silly love vow," Aunt Ester said, and smacked her lips.

"They shouldn't? Well, this feller . . . I mean, what can he do? He pure hates this girl with a heavy passion and —"

"He can tell the truth, that's what he can do. Honesty is the best policy."

"But, what if the girl don't want to hear honesty? What if she's as stubborn as nine kinds of mules and — "

"Then she's a fool! A girl that don't want a boy to be honest with her is even worse than a fool. She's an idiot!" Aunt Ester snapped and turned back to her pot and started scrubbing and singing again.

I left the kitchen and walked quietly through the front room so I wouldn't wake Uncle Clayborn snoozing on the divan, and went out on the porch and sat down. It was turning dark and a wind was whipping down through the trees and blowing across the porch. It was cool and soothing to my weary mind. I had a lot to think about. It seemed to me that Uncle Jack and Adeline and Aunt Ester was all right in what they said, to some degree, but it looked like I was going to have to sift through it all and come up with my own answer. I sighed deeply, thinking about the heavy burden of what I had to do. Somehow it seemed I'd of rather took a bite out of a mean old snake than tell Sylvie Bogart I didn't love her.

I wished Bear was there with me. Bear would know just what to say to a girl like Sylvie. He'd know for sure and for certain. I looked out across the yard and into the field next to the house and watched the branches of the big old pine trees whip back and forth in the wind. They swished and swooped and sounded like eerie whispers. I tilted my head and listened hard, trying to make out what the wind could be saying. After a little while, it come to me that the words were "Taffy . . . Taffy . . . Taffy . . ." over and over again, and I felt a chill of sadness rush through me.

15
A New Singing Teacher Comes to Town

"Have you seen the new singing teacher, Clayborn?" Aunt Ester asked Uncle Clayborn when he was just about dozed off on the divan.

"What's new about her?" Uncle Clayborn asked drowsily.

"What's *new* about her? Miss Benson's gone and *she's* what's new!" Aunt Ester exploded. "Where have you been all your born days, anyway?" Uncle Clayborn twisted restlessly on the divan and Aunt Ester snapped, "I swear, Clayborn Tarver, if you had a brain, you'd be a danger! Lay there and sleep your life away like an old hound dog after the hunt!"

Uncle Clayborn cracked his eyes apart and looked across the room at Aunt Ester where she was sitting in her rocking chair doing embroidery work on a tea towel. "Now, Essie," he said. "I ain't asleep. I been laying right here listening to every word that come out of your sweet mouth."

Aunt Ester was so busy with her head bent over her tea towel that she didn't hear Uncle Clayborn whisper to me, "What did she say, boy?"

I was sitting on the floor reading my new adventure book and leaning against the divan where Uncle Clayborn laid, so I could hear his whisper real good. "She asked, did you meet the new singing teacher," I whispered out of the side of my mouth behind my book, while watching Aunt Ester under my eyebrows.

Uncle Clayborn cleared his throat. "No, Essie," he said, "I ain't met ner seen the new singing teacher. Where do she hail from?"

"That I don't know. But she's got an odd name."

"What's her name?" Uncle Clayborn asked, looking like he was near about ready to sink back into his snooze.

"Fleur Portune."

"Humm . . . Fleur . . . that is an odd handle," Uncle Clayborn said with his eyes fluttering closed.

"It's French, I reckon." Aunt Ester looked up with a frown. "Seems like I heard that name before, but I can't rightly remember where," Aunt Ester said, and she looked back down at her embroidery work.

The words I was reading in my book froze in my eyes. I stared at them hard, trying to make them move, but they was froze into a solid blur and wouldn't budge. I tried not to cough, tried not to draw any attention to me, but I started gagging and coughing like I was in a spasm and couldn't stop.

Aunt Ester looked across at me and asked, "What's wrong, boy?"

"N-nothing . . ." I sputtered, and suddenly a heavy whack pounded across my back.

"That'll help," Uncle Clayborn said.

"Go take a swaller of water," Aunt Ester told me, and I got up and out of there quick.

That name! Fleur! Could it be? I wondered. No, I told myself, there was lots of women named Fleur . . . but . . . I'd never heard of no one with that name except . . . except down at the pond where we found Miracle! My heart started pounding so hard I could hear it in my ears. At the kitchen sink I pumped up some water in a cup like I was in a fury and swallered it down in one big gulp.

"Better now, Lyon?" Aunt Ester called out.

"Y-yes, m-ma'am," I called back.

"Good. Now you better get a move on and get them horses fed before time to go to church," Uncle Clayborn called.

I'd almost forgot it was Sunday, after hearing that Fleur name. I hurried out and fed Miss Pitty-Pat and Rhett and Scarlett as fast I could so I wouldn't be late, but, like always, Aunt Ester was already gunning the Chevy's engine impatiently, and I just had time to jump into the back seat before she sped off down the road in a whirl of dust and chicken cluckings.

In church I tried to stop trembling, but it was all I could do to keep from falling to pieces. I couldn't keep still. I felt like a hundred million ants was crawling around in my britches and couldn't get out. When the congregation was called on to stand and sing, I was the first one up and so glad to get shut of my tension that I bellered out the words to the hymn like I was calling hogs, and Aunt Ester laid her hand on my shoulder and frowned down at me.

Adeline sat on the other side of Aunt Ester holding Miracle in her lap. He seemed to be getting bigger and more lively every time I seen him. His big blue eyes swept all around the room, looking at everyone and everything, while his little curled fists moved a mile a minute from poking in and out of his mouth, to what looked liked swatting flies. Adeline kept a smile going in his direction all the time. I got a big lump in my throat just thinking about how much she loved that baby and all the things Sylvie was threatening and I just couldn't get that Fleur name out of my mind.

After the singing was over and preacher Dawson started up his sermon, I looked all around, thinking maybe I'd see the new singing teacher. My eyes spun up and down every row, front and back, but all I saw was the same familiar Sunday faces. By the time the service was over, I felt like them ants was having another traffic jam in my britches. I couldn't wait to get out of there!

Everyone was standing around in the church-yard when Justin come up to me, yanked me by my arm, and pulled me down the steps whispering, "Lyon, I got something to tell you!"

Justin didn't have to tell me he'd heard the

name of the new singing teacher too. I knew from the expression on his face. But as soon as he started to mention it, his mama called from across the churchyard, standing beside the family car.

"Hurry along now, Justin! We got to get home for our company!"

As soon as Justin left, I spotted Taffy in her white Sunday dress and little old lacy gloves and yeller straw hat walking by herself. I ran toward her, calling her name. She turned and tossed her long braid back over her shoulder. I sure got a different feeling looking at Taffy than I did when I looked at Sylvie.

"Taffy," I said when I reached her, "have you got a new singing teacher?" I was hoping she would tell me all she knew about Fleur Portune.

Instead she frowned at me and snapped, "What do you care?"

"I . . . well, I was just wondering, that's all. I heard Miss Benson went away . . ."

"Miss Benson got hitched up to some old fly-by-nighter over to Tylersville that don't have a dime!" Taffy said and give her braid another toss like I was a fly and she wanted to brush me away, and started sashaying along the long row of oleander bushes that grow at the side of the churchyard. She started plucking off the pink petals of the poison flowers as she walked.

"Wait, Taffy!" I said, follering quick behind her. "What's your new singing teacher like? What's her name?"

Taffy turned and exploded with a disgusted

sigh, screwed up her mouth, and give me a hard, impatient look out of her dark eyes. "Why are you so all of a sudden interested in the new singing teacher, Lyon? You never cared a diddly-darn about Miss Benson."

"I . . . well, I was just wondering, that's all. A feller's got a right to be curious," I said, feeling embarrassed. I looked down at my Sunday shoes and a pink petal was caught in the laces of one of them.

"You know what curiosity did, Lyon Savage?" Taffy said as she tossed a petal at me. "It killed a cat, that's what it did!"

I shoved my hands into my pockets and follered Taffy along the oleander bushes, feeling like the fool she thought I was, and wishing she would stop wearing that pretty white dress with the ruffles and lace on it that she wore every Sunday, and stop wearing them lacy white gloves with her fingers sticking out the little holes, and stop wearing that yeller straw hat that made my eyes ache just to look at her.

"You sure are something, Lyon! Asking about that new singing teacher like as if you wanted to take lessons yourself," Taffy said, and looked around and tossed another petal at me along with a smirking smile. "You know you only used that as an excuse to talk to me because you ain't got the gumption to think of no other way to start a conversation with me." She tossed another petal at me and it landed between my jacket collar and shirt.

I was something, all right, to let Taffy keep

throwing them flower petals at me and just keep on follering her. Looked like I was a fool for sure.

When we reached the end of the yard and the place where the oleander bushes stopped, the Bogarts' old Ford drove past with Justin and Sylvie hanging out the back winder. "Are you coming to our weenie roast, Lyon?" Sylvie yelled at me. But the car sped on by before I could yell back.

"Well, are you?" Taffy asked, and she flipped around, swinging that braid again, and started sashaying back up into the yard alongside the oleander bushes, jerking and pulling at the flowers.

"Maybe. I don't know," I told her, follering behind her and watching the ruffles sway on the tail of her skirt.

"Oh, you dumb old boys, anyway! It's always 'maybes' and 'sort ofs' and 'I'll think about it'! Don't you know how to say plain old *yes*?" Taffy cried like she was mad at me all of a sudden, and, turning around and glaring at me, she tossed a handful of petals in my face. Before they could even fall off, she had flounced away and was hurrying across the churchyard.

"Don't you know oleander flowers is poison, you dumb old girl?" I shouted, I was so mad, and several people standing around near the church turned and stared at me.

Taffy turned around and shouted back at me, "Good! Maybe you'll eat some!"

"Prissy old stupid girl, anyway!" I grumbled as I slapped the petals off my shoulders and out of my hair and collar. But I couldn't help watching Taffy's skirt swinging and her legs moving and her braid bouncing as she ran up the steps of the church.

Late that afternoon, after a big dinner of fried chicken and roastin' ears and hot buttered biscuits and white-flour gravy made out of grease drippings and Aunt Ester's chocolate cake, Justin come over and we walked down to the pond to the very place where we found the baby. We set down on the bank and hung our feet over into the cool, almost clear water, and felt it ripple gently through our toes. It was pleasant sitting there except for the bad and sorrowful thoughts that paraded around in my brain as loud as the big band that plays in the park over to Tylersville on the Fourth of July. They ain't so good, but they sure are hard to shut out. Just like my thoughts.

"You coming to our weenie roast?" Justin asked.

"I reckon," I answered. Along with everything else, my mind was still in a plague of worry over how I was going to break the true-love vow with Sylvie. Justin, being Sylvie's brother, I decided it best not to mention it to him. Some things you have to keep private. Even from your best friend.

"You reckon that new singing teacher is Miracle's mother, Lyon?" Justin asked as he swished his toes around in the water.

"I don't know," I said, watching the water ripple over my feet, "but if she is and she sees Adeline with that baby, we're going to catch old-billy-hell for sure. And not only that, when Bear comes back . . ."

Justin looked up at me. "Bear coming back ought to be the least of our worries right now. He's far enough away not to let what happens in Clement's Pond bother him."

"Bear ain't going to forget what the Gypsy told him, no matter how far away he goes! Soon as he gets back, the first thing he'll be wanting to know is who them people was that put the baby on Adeline's porch.

"Any way you look at it, Adeline is going to lose. If that singing teacher turns out to be Miracle's mother, she loses. If Sylvie takes the baby, she loses. When Bear comes back and the Gypsy tells him who started this whole durned dumb mess, she loses," I said, and I would of jumped right into the pond then and there except I knew I'd catch what Uncle Clayborn called "hell personified" from Aunt Ester for getting my clothes all wet. I bent over and dropped my chin into my hands and stared out over the pond. I got a gander of Justin out of the corner of my eye. He had dropped his chin into his hands too. Reckon we looked like two bumps on a log with the birds twittering over our heads in the tree branches.

After a while Justin said, "What you reckon Adeline would do if she lost the baby, Lyon?"

"Die," I told him. "She'd die as dead as if she was one of our old roosters runned over by Aunt Ester's Chevy!"

Justin shook his head and swished his feet

again. "She wouldn't believe in the Lord no more, that's for sure."

"I reckon not," I said, and I couldn't say another word. My throat was all closed up tight like my voice was locked behind a heavy door and couldn't come out.

16
Sylvie Does
the Unbelievable

Justin and Sylvie had dug a big round hole in
their backyard and put pine needles and twigs
and dry leaves in it and set a fire to going and
that's where we roasted the weenies. First we
put them on long sticks we pulled out of the
peach tree and sharpened into points at one end.
Then we all sat around the hole of fire and held
the sticks with the weenies on them in the flame
until they sizzled. When a dark crust formed on
them, they was ready to eat.

Me and Justin and Fulton Kramer and Mercy
McCloud and T-Roy Tate and Taffy and Sylvie
ate two hot dogs each, then Sylvie jumped up
and said, "We got marshmellers, too!" And she
run and got the sack and we all stuck five or six
on the ends of our sticks and T-Roy yelled, "Y'all
guys better let them cool off before you put them
in your mouth!"

"Oh, shoot! You're so askeered you'll hurt
your little old silly tongue!" Sylvie said, and she

took her stick out of the fire and yanked one of the dripping marshmellers off and shoved it right into her mouth. Then, all of a sudden, her eyes got big and wide and she screamed and spit out the marshmeller and beat a path over to the table where the big pitcher of punch was, while everyone laughed at her good and hard.

"Big brave girl!" Fulton snickered. "Thought you'd show us, didn't you now?"

"Thought was the thought that only thought it could!" I said.

"Y'all hush up!" Sylvie yelled between big gulps of punch.

"You better quit that showing off, Sylvie," Fulton laughed, letting us see the place where his teeth used to be. "Burning your tongue was just the Lord's way of — "

"Oh, no!" we all groaned. It sounded like Fulton was getting ready to go to preaching again.

When everything settled down, Mercy said, "Taffy's got a new song."

"Taffy's always got a new song!" T-Roy said with a grin.

"My new singing teacher, Miss Fleur Portune, taught me a beautiful song and I'd sing it if I had a mind to," Taffy said.

"You mean you'd sing it if you was *asked* to," Justin said with a wink and a snicker. Everyone laughed and Taffy started pounding her fists into Justin's arm.

"You going to let Taffy get away with that?" Fulton asked, chuckling.

Taffy stopped pounding on Justin and said,

"You old boys make me sick! They got nice boys over to Tylersville. Real educated and fine-mannered boys. Miss Fleur told me. They play the pianola and dance like movie stars."

"Then why don't you go over there and get you one!" T-Roy laughed.

"I aim to. When I get growed up That's just what I aim to do. I'll be a singer then. I might even be a movie star."

"Says who?" T-Roy asked with a grin.

"Says *me*, that's who," Taffy snapped, with her hands on her hips and her eyes flashing.

"I see an old baseball over yonder! Let's play catch!" Mercy said, and she jumped up and ran to get the ball. Everyone except me and Sylvie follered her and started tossing the ball back and forth between them.

I turned and looked at Sylvie. She was just sitting there, looking down into the fire in the hole. This was my chance to tell her what I had dreaded telling her. It was my chance, but I was so nervous I would of rather wrestled with Oscar Bebee's old bull! I took a deep breath and said as gently as I knew how:

"Sylvie, I been wanting to talk to you about something." I stopped and studied her face in the low fire glow. She was all silvery blond and white and shining and glowing, just like the moon. But I had something to say and no moonlight was going to stop me.

"I thought you'd done said all you had to say," she said into the fire. "But I'm listening."

I cleared my throat and took another deep breath. "Sylvie, it's about that true-love vow . . ."

"I figured it was," she snapped.

"I been wanting to tell you what I'm going to say ever since that first time you said all them things about taking Miracle away from Adeline . . ." Sylvie looked up out of the fire at me. "What you said . . . all them mean threats . . . well, they made me stop and think . . ."

"Think what?" Sylvie's voice sounded suspicious.

"About us. About what we said in that true-love vow. Well, what I'm trying to say is, I want to . . . that is, I'd like to . . . no, what I mean is, I *want* to withdraw my vow that I made you." Sylvie cut in with a deep, deep sigh. A sigh that sounded like she was surprised and hurt at the same time. But I couldn't stop now. "I want to take it all back because . . . well, because I don't think you and me is . . . is suited for each other." I could feel the hot sweat popping out all over me when I got done saying all that.

Sylvie just stared at me with the last glow from the fire flickering across her face. She looked all changed now, like her features belonged to someone else and I was sitting there with a complete stranger. The laughter and noise the kids was making in the yard didn't seem to fit in with me and Sylvie. I wished I hadn't said it then and there, after all. I wished I could of said it gentler. Looked like there wasn't no gentle way to take back a vow from a girl, though.

Unexpectedly, Sylvie stood up and looked down at me like she hated the very sight of me. "You'll be sorry, Lyon Savage!" she said evenly.

"You'll be the sorriest boy in the county!" Then she turned, scooting dirt up over my hand where it rested on the ground, and hurried away.

I watched her join in with the others and start shouting and laughing and throwing the ball just like as if nothing had ever happened. Just like as if she wasn't mad ner hurt ner anything. A little while later, though, I found out what she meant when she said I'd be sorry. Everyone was helping clean up things and making sure nothing was left around on the ground for Mrs. Bogart to get mad about. I picked up the weenie and marshmeller sticks and took them to the big burning barrel at the edge of the yard and started to drop them in when, close by, behind a clump of scrub pine, I heard Sylvie's words as plain as day. I wouldn't of even cared to listen except I couldn't help it when I heard Adeline's name mentioned.

"That baby Adeline Newberry claims the Lord left on her porch with his own hands wasn't no such of a thing!" she said, and my heart leapt into my mouth and I started shaking all over.

She had promised! Me and her and Justin had all promised on the night we took the baby to Adeline's that we'd never tell a word of what we done. Now Sylvie was telling it! She was telling it and only the Lord in heaven knew what would happen next!

"How do you know?" It was Taffy's voice!

"I know because it was me and Justin and

Lyon Savage who found that baby and put it on Adeline's porch!" Sylvie answered right up.

I heard Taffy catch her breath in a loud gasp and say, "That ain't true, Sylvie!"

"Oh, yes it is! We found that baby down by the pond in the underbrush, and if we hadn't come along and took it away from there, the rain would of washed it right into the pond and it would of drowned." I heard Taffy gasp again and Sylvie cautioned, "Don't you say a word about this, Taffy. We'd get skinned alive if anyone found out."

"Oh, you don't have to worry about me, Sylvie. You know I'd never tell a thing like that on my best friend," Taffy insisted, but something in her voice made me think different.

"I was counting on taking that baby myself," Sylvie went on in a voice prickled with anger and bitterness. "But I don't want it now. Lyon broke the true-love vow he made with me. I was going to make that little baby *our* baby. His and mine. Now I wouldn't have it!"

If everything else hadn't been so terrible, I would of fell over with happiness at what Sylvie said about not wanting the baby anymore. But all I could do was stand there and tremble in my brogans. Could she of really been thinking of Miracle as mine and hers? I shook all the more, just to think of such a crazy thing. Fact is, I don't think I'd ever heard anything more crazy in all my born days!

Like as not, Sylvie would have said more but Zooie come charging up and said, "Sylvie, your mama wants you to go in the house and chop some more ice for the punch."

"Oh, that old ice pick always hurts my hand!" Sylvie complained.

"You better go on," Zooie told her, "or your mama will be out here with a switch and make you go!"

I heard Sylvie stomp off and she no more than got out of earshot when Taffy started in with Zooie. I couldn't believe what I was hearing. It seemed like I was having a nightmare. "Mama, you know how I been wanting another doll for my collection — "

"I don't want to talk about no dolls, Taffy Marshall! You been so ornery lately, I may never buy you another doll," Zooie cut her off.

"Not even if I tell you the most *secret* secret of all secrets?"

"What do you mean, 'the most *secret* secret of all secrets'?" Zooie asked suspiciously, and my heart near about jumped out of my chest.

"You got to promise me you'll get me that Spanish Señorita doll, mama. The one with the sequins on the dress and the fancy combs in her hair and — "

"All right, Taffy. I reckon I'll have to or die of curiosity," Zooie said with a disgusted-sounding sigh and I couldn't stand it any longer. I dropped the sticks and bag into the burning barrel and hightailed it out of that yard feeling just like J. Edgar Hoover and the whole FBI was at my heels. Everyone started yelling at me to come back, but I just kept going. Sylvie was right when she said I'd be sorry for breaking the true-love vow with her. Truer words was never spoken.

When I got home I was so filled up with emotion that I couldn't go in the house. Instead I went around to the back pasture where Miss Pitty-Pat was standing. There she was, a dark shadow against the sky that looked like a statue. I run up to her and she didn't do a thing but keep on standing there, like a queen, like she deserved to be hugged, knowing I loved her just about as much as anyone could love an old do-nothing mare. I reached up and put my arms around her long, sloping neck and pressed my face into her and started babbling and crying at the same time.

"Oh, Miss Pitty-Pat . . ." She nuzzled her head up close to me and blinked her eyes like she was understanding everything I was saying to her. "It's all our fault that Adeline has that baby . . . all our fault she thinks the Lord put it on her porch. Now . . . now that Fleur woman has come to town and . . . and wh-what if . . . what if she's the baby's mother and . . . and, oh, we should of took that baby to the police . . . now Sylvie's gone and told Taffy Marshall what we done and Taffy's told her mama and now everyone is going to be hurt . . . and Bear . . . Bear won't never trust me again!" I couldn't go on because I was crying so hard. I hung on to Miss Pitty-Pat's neck like I was lost in a whirling sea and she was my anchor. There wasn't no one else I could tell all this to but Miss Pitty-Pat.

"Lyon! You out there, boy?" Aunt Ester's voice rushed across the pasture from the house.

I let go of Miss Pitty-Pat and sniffled back my tears and swiped my nose on my shirt sleeve and hollered, "I'm down here in the pasture with Miss Pitty-Pat."

"Leave that old mare be and get up here to the house and get your chores done!" The back door slammed shut with a hard bang.

I give Miss Pitty-Pat a final hug and run off to the house. Soon as I opened the door Aunt Ester said, "Boy, I thought you was at the Bogarts'."

"I was," I told her, "but I got a . . . I got a headache and come home."

"Did I hear you out there crying to old Miss Pitty-Pat?" Aunt Ester asked, looking over her glasses at me.

"Crying? Who? Me?" My throat was so stuffed up with crying lumps that I could hardly talk.

"Come over here under the light and let me look at you." I went. No point in holding back. "You been crying, ain't you, boy?" Aunt Ester said. I sniffled. I couldn't help it. "It's because of Bear, ain't it? Oh, he never should of went away this time. Couldn't he see his boy growing up and needing him?" Aunt Ester grabbed me then and put her arms around me and I wished with all my heart that it was Bear being gone again that was making me cry.

17
What Zooie Did
with the Secret Secret

She come out of Goad's store and the minute I
seen her, I knew she was Miracle's mother. She
stood in front of the store for a second, looking
up and down, like she was wondering which way
to go. It was Saturday and the town was full of
shoppers, people passed in front of her, going
in and out of the stores.

"Oh, look, Lyon, there's the new singing
teacher," Aunt Ester said, and she took off
across the street and straight up to Fleur
Portune.

I follered Aunt Ester, carrying some of her
packages, and staring at Fleur Portune all the
way. When we reached her, I could see her eyes
was the exact same color as Miracle's, and I had
to catch my breath because she was so beautiful.
Her hair was long and practically the same color
of my mother's hair in the picture I had of her.
Her lips was plump and rosy and she made a
sweet smile when she said hello to Aunt Ester.

In what Aunt Ester called my "heart of hearts" I couldn't understand how a woman who looked so like an angel could of left her baby in danger.

"You're the new singing teacher, ain't you?" Aunt Ester said in a friendly way. "You took Miss Benson's place."

"Yes, that's so, ma'am," Fleur Portune answered, and her voice was as sweet as a sugar-coated breeze. It made me wish she'd talk a blue streak, just so I could keep listening.

"I'm Ester Tarver and this here is my nephew, Lyon Savage. But don't let his name fool you, he's as tame as a little kitten," Aunt Ester said, and she put out her hand and shook Fleur Portune's soft, delicate-looking hand. Then she give me a nudge and said, "Speak up, boy. Where's your manners? Don't go giving the new singing teacher the wrong impression."

"Hello, Lyon." Fleur smiled and put her hand out to shake mine.

"Hello, ma'am," I said, and when her skin touched mine, I didn't think I'd ever felt anything so warm and soft.

"I been wanting to ask you to tea one of these days," Aunt Ester said, "but seems like a body can't never get all the things done that need to get done, so's they can give an invite to someone. I reckon you'll be taking over all Miss Benson's duties. She always presided over the young people's meetings. Maybe you could come to tea next Saturday, Miss Portune. I could send my husband, Clayborn, in the Chevy to pick you up."

I didn't think Aunt Ester would ever run

down, but when she did, Fleur Portune said, "I'm sorry, Mrs. Tarver, but I'm giving lessons on that day. Perhaps another time."

"Yes . . . well . . . hummm," Aunt Ester said, pursing her lips. "Good day, Miss Portune."

"Good day, Mrs. Tarver. Good-bye, Lyon," Fleur said with another smile. "It was very nice meeting you."

"The pleasure was ours," Aunt Ester told her, and when we walked away, all I could think about was how beautiful and soft-spoken Fleur was.

"What's got into you, boy?" Aunt Ester barked, "I've asked you three times already to take this here sack!"

I looked up, half-expecting to see Fleur Portune's beautiful face staring down at me. I winced when I saw that it was Aunt Ester, with her glasses slid halfway down of her nose!

"I'll swanee, you are a sight, Lyon Savage! I reckon you need a good tonic . . ."

"Oh, no . . . no, Aunt Ester, I don't need a tonic! Honest! I'm fine. Just fine," I said real quick, while I grabbed the sack out of her hands and rushed across the road to the Chevy. When we were on our way home, I asked, "Did you think she was beautiful, Aunt Ester?"

"Who?" Aunt Ester said as we swung around a corner at her usual neck-breaking speed.

"Miss Portune," I answered, hanging on to the sack like as if it could keep me from falling out of the seat.

"Oh . . . her. Never hit a lick of work in her born days! Hands like a baby's skin. Never chopped a field of cotton ner scrubbed a wood floor ner pounded a nail with a splintery hammer ner washed clothes on a rub board, and never will, I'll vow. Not a blister ner nary a callus on them fine hands."

"But did you think she was beautiful?"

Aunt Ester's face softened. "That I did, boy. As beautiful as your own dear mother, Lord rest her pure and decent soul."

Just as we made the turn to go into the yard Aunt Ester yelped, "I *knowed* I'd heard that woman's name before! You mentioned it to me, Lyon!"

While the chickens flew up out of the way of the Chevy and cackled for their lives, and the dust soared up from the wheels of the car, I gulped so hard I felt like I'd pulled my tonsils all the way down my throat and into my belly! Aunt Ester braked the Chevy in a sizzle of dust and flying chickens and turned to give me a look that said *more* than curious. "How come you to know that singing teacher's name, boy?" Aunt Ester's eyes was like hawk's eyes, staring over her glasses at me.

"Miss Fleur's name, Aunt Ester?" I opened the car door and jumped out fast.

"Well, I ain't talking about the president!" Aunt Ester snapped as she got out of the car. "That's a plumb odd name," she muttered as she pulled bags out of the car and handed them to me.

When I saw the pickup truck come rattling into the yard, I thought I was saved. But I could tell from the way it was driving and the way the wheels screeched that I wasn't saved from nothing. It was Zooie Marshall driving that pickup like she was hell-bent for fury! Thing was, I'd been wondering just how long it would take her to get to Aunt Ester and tell her everything Taffy had told her. We no more than got into the house and set the groceries on the table before Zooie was jerking open the front door and shouting, "Ester! Ester Tarver!"

"Come on in, Zooie," Aunt Ester called from the kitchen, and under her breath she whispered, "As if you wasn't already in!"

Aunt Ester walked into the front room with me behind her, trying not to look into Zooie's eyes, and hoping she wouldn't see me. But she saw me, all right, and the first thing she said to Aunt Ester was, "Ester Tarver, I've got some things to tell you that you ought to know!" Her eyes was boring a hole into me as she spoke, and I started to shake all over.

"Sit down, Zooie," Aunt Ester told her as she pulled on her long apron. "Ain't no need to stand on ceremony."

"What I've got to say to you, I can say standing. But *you* better sit down, Ester." Zooie's eyes were as sharp and flashing as the corners on shattered glass.

Aunt Ester stared at Zooie a full minute before she backed over to her rocking chair and set down in it. Zooie smacked her lips good and loud, give me another cutting flash of her eyes, and started in.

Ain't no need to go into what all Zooie said about me and against me. Ain't no need to tell you about all the mean looks she give me ner the tears she made come into Aunt Ester's eyes ner all the shocked expressions she made come onto Aunt Ester's face. Ain't no need to tell all that ner that my legs was wobbling so bad that I felt, all the time Zooie was talking, that they'd buckle under me and I'd land face-first right in the floor. Ain't no need to tell how sorry I felt for Aunt Ester for raising a no-good useless kidnapping sprout like me! Ain't no use to go into any of that.

But when Zooie pointed her long, skinny finger at me and said, "He ain't no better than . . ." Aunt Ester jumped up and shouted, "Don't you go to calling my boy bad names, Zooie! I'll not tolerate that in my house!" Then Aunt Ester turned to me, and with a sad look on her face she said, "Lyon, now you heard what all Zooie here accused you of. And it ain't the first time you been accused of something by her. But won't do no good to stand before me and deny it iffen it's true. Now, iffen it ain't true, that's a horse of a different color — "

"Oh, it be true, all right!" Zooie cut in, and Aunt Ester give her a look that could of froze her stiff, even though it wasn't the dead of winter.

"Lyon . . ." Aunt Ester was waiting and looking at me like her heart was near about to breaking. "If you tell the truth, the Lord will smile down on you and send you some mighty big blessings, but if you don't tell the truth, for sure and for certain, you'll get a plague of damnation on you. Which would you rather have, boy?"

Before I could even get my mouth in gear to moving, Taffy come storming through the door and slamming it hard behind her. Her face was all red, like she'd been sitting out in the pickup crying.

"Mama, you promised me that Señorita doll for my collection if I told you my secret!" she cried, and Zooie turned around and grabbed her by her long braid and yelled, "Go on back out there to the truck before I lay into your hide!"

"Leave her alone!" I shouted, and I took a step forward, not even knowing what I might do, just dying inside because of the look on Taffy's face and the way Zooie was pulling at her braid, like as if she was going to yank it right out of Taffy's head.

"Don't you come at me like that, you little heathern!" Zooie yelled at me, and she give Taffy a big shove toward the door. Taffy broke away and ran out the door bawling so loud that the chickens in the yard started to cluck and the cow over in the next pasture begin to moo and, down in the corral, Miss Pitty-Pat and Rhett and Scarlett let out agitated whinnies.

"You ought not to treat that girl the way you do, Zooie," Aunt Ester told Zooie, and Zooie come back with, "And you ought to of raised that boy right, Ester Tarver! If you had, he wouldn't of tooken that baby and made poor old Adeline think the Lord give it to her!"

All the color washed out of Aunt Ester's face

then. It looked like all the puff and steam had drained right out of her and she collapsed back into her rocking chair. Zooie headed for the door and when she pushed it open, she looked back at me and spit, "You stay away from my girl, Lyon Savage! You hear me?" And out the door she went.

"Aunt Ester," I said after Zooie's pickup pulled out of the yard. But Aunt Ester didn't say a word, didn't even lift her head to look at me. She just stared down at her hands in the lap of her snow-white apron.

I went over and knelt down on my knees beside the rocking chair and said as gently as I could, "Aunt Ester, it's true what I done. But I didn't do it to hurt no one. Me and Justin and Sylvie, we did it so the baby wouldn't get pushed off into the pond by the rain and get drowned. We put him on Adeline's porch to protect him and to make Adeline happy. You know how much she wanted a little baby, and it was raining so hard . . ."

Aunt Ester reached up and touched my face with her rough hand. "What's going to happen to Adeline now, Lyon? How is she going to feel when she finds out it weren't the Lord who give her the little baby, but it was you children? How is she going to feel?"

I put my head down and bit hard into my lip. But that didn't keep me from crying. This wasn't what I wanted to happen. It was all wrong! If Adeline stopped believing in the Lord because of what I had a hand in doing, I knew I couldn't never face her again as long as I lived.

Fact of the matter is, I thought I might as well go down to the pond and throw myself right in!

I cried so hard my chest near about caved in from the pain and, all the time I was crying, Aunt Ester was rubbing my head with her hand and saying painfully, "Oh, Lord, what are we going to do? What are we going to do? . . ."

18
As Condemned
as a Mad Dog Killer

"You let me and this boy pass!" Aunt Ester
barked at the townspeople who stood around in
front of Goad's store blocking our way. Up and
down the street, people come to store winders
and peered out at the commotion or hurried up
to the crowd to get a gander at what was going
on.

"Now, Miss Ester," Oscar Bebee said after he
spit his tobaccer juice into the gutter. "Ain't
nobody got any quarrel with you . . ."

"Move out of my way, you tobaccer-spittin'
old fool!" Aunt Ester demanded. Oscar Bebee
give Aunt Ester a hard eye, but that didn't
stop her. "This here boy is a child of God and a
citizen of Clement's Pond and I want all of you
to remember that!" Aunt Ester went on as she
looked from face to face, challenging anyone
who refused to let us go into Goad's store.

"Now, you listen here," Oscar Bebee commenced again. "We ain't blaming you for what

Lyon and them Bogart young'uns done. We just got a pain in our hearts for what it's going to end up doing to old Adeline Newberry — "

"That's right," old man Lyman cut in from where he stood with his fingers tucked around the straps of his overalls. "If those kids'd gone to the police in the first place . . ."

Others in the crowd joined in with "That's right," and Aunt Ester reached out and sent old Oscar Bebee reeling from the sudden shove she give him. "Out of my way, you pesky tobaccer-spittin', judgmental asp!" Aunt Ester exploded, and everyone moved back, gasping in awe at what she had done, and made room for us to enter Goad's store. I was shuddering so bad I felt sure I'd never make it through that door, but somehow I did.

Soon as we got inside, Mr. Goad come up to us. "Howdo, Miss Ester. And you too, Lyon," he said, and I never saw his face looking so serious.

"If you got a judgment against this boy, speak it now, George Goad," Aunt Ester stated, glaring right into Mr. Goad's eyes. "I can always buy my goods over to Tylersville. Don't make no difference to me. My car can drive there same as it can drive here."

"I ain't got no judgment against no one, Miss Ester," Mr. Goad assured her. "No sireee. No judgment a'tall."

"Good. Then you can give me some . . ."

While Aunt Ester give Mr. Goad her order, I went over and stood beside a shelf of canned goods and started reading the labels on them.

Wasn't nothing else to do. I was as condemned as any mad-dog killer, it looked like. In the little time it took Zooie Marshall to spread the word all over town about what me and Justin and Sylvie done, there wasn't a person who didn't know all about it, inside and out, backwards and forwards and in between. The only good thing, so far as I could tell, was Sylvie hadn't mentioned Fleur's name after all. Leastways, I hadn't heard no gossip about Fleur Portune yet!

J. Edgar Hoover didn't come to arrest us, but it wasn't just Clement's Pond that knowed about Miracle no more. Mr. Cleetis Swafford, a special investigator from Tylersville, come to question us about Miracle and about what we'd done. Summer was coming on good with gardens growing like a fury and with huge sunflowers that hung over the fence and dandelions and daisies and sunshine popping out everywhere when Mr. Zeb Rice, the police chief of Clement's Pond, hauled us all down to the police station.

"Don't appear to me to be any malice intended here. Just a lot of dang fool poor judgment," Mr. Zeb Rice told Mr. Swafford.

"No," Mr. Swafford agreed, "there. don't seem to be no malice. However . . ."

Sylvie was all hung over, with her head in her lap, crying like she'd never stop, and Justin and me was running a heavy race to see who could shake the most. His face looked like he'd just eat a big red pepper, and my chin wouldn't stay still. When they brought Adeline and the baby in, I couldn't look straight at her. If I did, with her sitting there all stiff and prim in a hard-backed chair that Mr. Rice provided for her and holding Miracle in her arms like as if there wasn't hands strong enough to pry him away from her, I knowed I'd feel a hundred times worse, if that was possible.

"Miz Newberry, do you believe these two boys and this here towheaded girl to be rough-necks? Do you believe them to be wild and out of control?" Mr. Swafford asked Adeline and she looked him square in his eyes and said in a low, steady voice, "No, sir."

"You know we'll have to take the little feller from you — " Mr. Swafford said, and he no more than got the words out when Adeline jumped up, holding on to Miracle so tight the baby whimpered, and cried, "No! Please! No!"

Adeline got so hysterical, they had to call in Doc Gumble and the preacher to give her medicine and spiritual talking to. It seemed like the screaming and carrying on in that room went on for hours. And the more Adeline cried, the harder everyone cried. Finally, preacher Dawson said, "What would be the harm in letting this good Christian woman keep care of the little baby just until the real mother is found or you find some other place for him? What would it profit this here innocent little baby to be put in an orphanage when it's already used to good care and mothering from this kindhearted woman? I ask you, gentlemen?" And he was looking right at Mr. Swafford and Mr. Rice like he could wait all day for a logical answer and he wasn't going to leave that police station until he got it.

Mr. Swafford rubbed his chin like he had heavy thoughts crowding at his mind and Mr. Rice walked up and down the floor, frowning down at it like the answer was there in the floorboards, and all he had to do was find it. "Well . . ." Mr. Swafford said while he continued to rub his chin. "Well . . ."

We all stopped our moaning and crying and wailing and waited. No one in that room breathed while we waited. All you could hear was Mr. Rice's shoes going up and down the floor and letting out a little squeak every now and then. Aunt Ester reached over and pulled my hand into hers and held on to it and Mr. and Mrs. Bogart patted Sylvie and Justin on their shoulders, and even Miracle, bundled up in Adeline's arms, looked like he was holding his breath!

"Well," Mr. Swafford finally went on, "that might be a good temporary solution. We'll have to talk to the county case worker, of course."

Everyone started to cry and wail again, only with relief this time. But we soon hushed, when Mr. Swafford added, "You understand, Miz Newberry, you'll have to give this baby up when other accommodations are made for it."

"Yes, sir," Adeline said in a deep, sad voice.

"As for you children, I'm going to remand you over to your parents' care. I don't want you out running the streets or sneaking over to Tylersville for a good time. If you do, you're liable to *do* time!" There was such a stern look on Mr. Swafford's face, it made us all shiver.

"Yes, sir," me and Justin and Sylvie said in unison. I still couldn't look at Adeline.

But after all that was over, Adeline come up to us with Miracle gurgling in her arms. "You young'uns did the right thing in bringing Miracle to me," she said, her eyes still wet from crying. "It was a direction from the Lord hisself that made you choose me out of everyone else in Clement's Pond. I can't hold no grudge against a one of you." She looked around at Mr. Swafford and Mr. Rice and the other grownups and said, "It's a fact, all of you, that if these young'uns hadn't brought this baby to me, if they'd brought him to the police station, I never would of known the joy and love this tiny one has brought me. It was a miracle. And no matter what happens, I know my love has given him a good start in life." She bent her head and give Miracle a soft kiss on his forehead and he cooed and smiled as big as you please.

"That's mighty Christian of you to feel that way, Adeline," Mr. Bogart said, clearing his throat.

"Praise the Lord," Aunt Ester said, and Mrs. Bogart seconded the motion with a loud "Amen!"

"But . . . but what if the *true* mother comes and wants the baby?" Sylvie asked, and I almost fainted dead away for fear she was going to bring up the name I wished I could forget! Me and Justin exchanged a look and I could tell he was thinking the same thing I was.

Adeline looked down at Miracle and hugged

him close, like she was trying to protect him, but neither she ner anyone else in the room answered that question.

That same day, when me and Aunt Ester went to Goad's store to pick up things she'd forgot the last time she went, she took to talking to Mr. Goad right smart. "Seems like this town don't want to forget ner forgive these addlepated young'uns . . ." She had just got the last word out when the door opened and she let out a cry like she couldn't believe her own eyes. "Why, Ferdie Hughs!"

I snuck a good look around the canned-goods shelf where I was reading labels, and, sure enough, it was the same Ferdie Hughs that jilted Adeline Newberry all them years ago, looking older and more stoop-shouldered, but that was about all. Two raggedy-looking kids hung back behind him, peering around and gandering at Aunt Ester.

"How you be, Miss Ester?" Ferdie said with a wide jack-o'-lantern grin.

"What in the world are you doing back in Clement's Pond, Ferdie?" Aunt Ester asked, dropping her eyes to the two kids sneaking looks at her, then looking back at Ferdie.

"I come back to look for a place, Miss Ester," Ferdie answered.

"A place? What kind of place?"

"To live and work on. For me and my two young'uns here," Ferdie said, reaching back and pulling the two boys up beside him. They was so dirty and their hair was so long and stringy, it looked like they never had took up a good friendship with soap and water.

"Well, where's your wife, Ferdie?" Aunt Ester asked, eyeing the two dirty kids.

"Ma's gone to heaven," one of the boys answered.

"The Lord took her home," the other one said.

"Oh, my word!" Aunt Ester said, looking crumple-faced.

"Ferdie Hughs! As I live and breathe, it's really you!" Mr. Goad said as he stuck out his hand and went to pumping Ferdie's hand up and down.

"How you be, George?" Ferdie asked, grinning his jack-o'-lantern grin again.

"Well, ain't you got two fine boys!" Aunt Ester said, smiling at the boys.

"This'un is Skeeter," Ferdie said, pushing the one with the longest, dirtiest hair out in front of him. "And this'un is Huey."

"How would you boys like a peppermint candy?" Mr. Goad asked, and went right to the candy jar.

When we left Goad's store, Ferdie and his two boys went with us. Aunt Ester cooked up a meal that looked like Thanksgiving had arrived early, and the way them two kids and old Ferdie went after it, you'd of swore they hadn't had a meal in a month. No one ever did mention Adeline Newberry the whole time. But I reckon no one had forgot how old Ferdie had jilted her. After supper was over, Uncle Clayborn and

Ferdie pushed all the furniture out of the way in the front room and laid down quilts for him and the boys to sleep on. We sure had a houseful that night. Seemed like Aunt Ester and Uncle Clayborn and old Ferdie was running a race to see who could snore the loudest and the longest. I reckon Aunt Ester won out, though.

19
I Get an Unexpected
Promise from Bear

"Geeeeehaaaaaaa!"

The wild cry come hurling down the road like a tornado while I was out on the front steps carving a toy horse out of wood for Skeeter and Huey. I looked up and listened.

"What's that?" Skeeter and Huey asked at the same time, and looked down the road with their ears popped up and their eyes popped out.

"It's Bear!" I yelled. "It's my daddy!" I dropped my carving knife and the piece of wood and took off toward the road. I couldn't believe it was Bear already. It hadn't been six months yet. It hadn't even been four months.

"Geeeeehaaaaaaa!" It came again and I was ready, priming myself to run and jump right into Bear's big arms as soon as I got sight of him. There he was all at once, running down the road through the dust with the afternoon sun caught in his hair, laughing and yelling and looking like he'd never left.

"It ain't been six months, Bear!" I shouted as I ran to him. "It ain't been six months!"

Bear hugged me and laughed. "You reckon I ought to turn around and head back?" he asked, and I shouted, "No! No, Bear!" as I burrowed my head deep into his neck.

It sure didn't set well with Bear when he learned from Aunt Ester and Uncle Clayborn what had happened and my part in it with the baby. At the supper table Bear glowered over me with heavy, stern eyes that made me feel like I was shriveling up into a tiny little prune.

"All that true, boy, what your Aunt Ester and Uncle Clayborn say?" he barked at me like he was ready at any second to snap my head right off my shoulders.

"Fess up, Lyon," Uncle Clayborn prodded me. "Telling the truth has saved more backsides than one from a sitting-down pain."

Bear continued to stare at me like watching my P's and Q's wouldn't do a bit of good. The damage was already done.

"Well?" Bear asked again, looking like he was ready to reach across the table and swipe my head right off.

"Y-yes, sir," I answered with a thick lump in my throat that wouldn't go down when I swallered my mashed pertaters.

"Leave the boy be, Bear," Aunt Ester said. "The young'uns made Adeline the happiest woman this town has ever seen, and saw that the baby didn't drowned."

Made her happy, then made her miserable, I thought guiltily.

Ferdie looked up from his piled-high plate. "Adeline . . . Adeline Newberry?" His eyes got as big and as round as Aunt Ester's washtub that hung on a nail outside the back door.

Uncle Clayborn jumped right in, telling all the details about what had happened, and Ferdie stared at Uncle Clayborn all the time he was chewing. I never saw no one eat as much as Ferdie Hughs could and stay so skinny.

"Adeline was always a good woman," Ferdie said when Uncle Clayborn stopped telling everything.

"Why don't you take the young'uns and go and pay a call on Adeline, Ferdie?" Aunt Ester suggested. "Adeline ain't got no grudge in her heart for you marrying someone else. Especially when she sees your two fine motherless boys, she won't."

Ferdie frowned. "I don't reckon I could do that, Miss Ester," he said, shaking his head and getting ready to stab another green bean with his fork.

"Why, Addie would feel plumb robbed of pleasure if you didn't take those motherless boys over to visit her," Aunt Ester went on.

"Well . . . I'll rest on it, Miss Ester," Ferdie said like as if he only wanted to appease Aunt Ester. But it looked plain that seeing Adeline Newberry was about the last thing he wanted to do. I reckon he felt mighty guilty for running out on her the way he done.

"We'll have ourselves a fine big talk after supper, boy," Bear said gruffly, and I gulped and looked down into my plate real quick. I wondered if that fine big talk included a switch from off the peach tree!

I was already in bed when Bear come into the room and said my name. I was all scrunched down under my quilt with my face turned to the wall.

"No need to pretend you're asleep, Lyon. I've been a possum player all my life. I know another one when I see one," Bear said, and I opened my eyes and turned to face him. He was looking me square in my face. I couldn't keep from trembling, he looked so fierce. "So the old hunchback Gypsy was right, after all," he went on. "There really was three of you."

"Y-yes, sir," I managed to confess without choking.

"Why didn't you tell me, Lyon, instead of letting me think and wonder and worry it all up in my mind the way I done? Why didn't you tell me what you and the Bogart young'uns done? It would of saved us all a passel of trouble."

"I wanted to! Honest, Bear! But I reckon . . . I reckon I was too askeered to."

Bear sat down on the edge of the bed. "That's one thing you don't have to be, Lyon. You don't ever have to be afraid of telling your own daddy anything. Look what your being afraid has done." He dropped his head and started rubbing his chin like he was thinking some mighty heavy thoughts. After a minute or two he looked up and back at me. "Well, I reckon me not being around all these years for you to learn to tell things to and share things with has made this as much my fault as yours."

You don't have to take no blame, Bear! I wanted to shout, but he hurried on before I could get my mouth ready to speak. "That's all over, though," he said. "I aim to be around and underfoot from now on, boy. I aim to do the right things by you from now on."

I sat up stiff and straight and stared at Bear. "What do you mean?"

"I mean, I'm back for good this time . . ."

I couldn't even wait for Bear to finish. I jumped up and threw my arms around his neck and hung on. "How come you decided, Bear? How come?"

"You decided it for me just now, son. There's no way under the sun I could go away now and leave you to face whatever comes up in the future over what you and the Bogart young'uns done." Bear started rubbing his hand over my back. "And I guess it's high time I quit my gallivanting, anyway. After a time a man gets plumb wore out of roaming."

"But what about your partner, Bear? What about your commitment?"

"The whole deal fell through. That partner of mine turned out to be about as uncommitted as any rascal could be, and more interested in liquor than in settling down to business," Bear answered. "But I guess, like the feller says, experience is the best teacher." Bear pulled away from me then and looked me right in my eyes. "You learned by this 'miracle-baby' experience, boy?" he asked gruffly.

"Oh, I swear it, Bear! I have. Yes, sir, I have.

I ain't *never* going to do a thing like this again as long as I live!"

After we put the lamp out and Bear was in bed beside me I said, "Bear, I sure wish that Adeline could keep that baby forever and ever."

"Little chance of that, Lyon. The law will probably find a place for him in the city."

"You mean . . . you mean . . . a p-place like the county orphans' home?"

"I reckon that's where they put children like Miracle," Bear said sleepily. "Children that don't have no mother."

I swallered so hard the sound thundered in my ears like a gong, and thought about Fleur Portune. Suddenly I wanted to tell Bear about her and about hearing the "Fleur" the night we found the baby by the pond. "Bear?" I said, but he didn't answer. "Bear?" I said again, and he let out a big snore. He was already asleep!

"Bear!" I whispered one more time into the darkness. But his snore told me he wasn't about to wake up for man ner beast. Suddenly I felt as askeered for Miracle's mama as I did for myself!

20
Bear Meets Fleur

We were just crossing the road heading for the pond to do some fishing when Fleur Portune come down the walk on the other side carrying some books. Bear nearly fell in his tracks gandering at her.

"That's the new singing teacher," I told him.

"If her voice is as pretty as she is, she has got to be an angel," Bear said, still gandering like as if he was looking at the most beautiful thing he'd ever laid his eyes on.

On the other side of Bear, Aunt Ester laughed and said, "You stay around the house for the young people's meeting tonight and you'll find out."

"I may just do that, Ester," Bear said, watching Fleur go around a corner and out of sight.

It struck me again how much Fleur Portune and little Miracle resembled each other. And I knew for sure and for certain if Miss Fleur Portune was Miracle's mother, she couldn't live in Clement's Pond and not hear all the talk buzzing night and day about Miracle and Adeline. She would have to be blind or deaf or both. You sure couldn't tell what was going on behind that pretty face of hers. But if I was right and she was the Fleur that left Miracle at the pond that night, why didn't she go to Adeline and tell her? I wondered. Wouldn't she at least want to get a gander at the baby? Why else would she be back in Clement's Pond? And if she wasn't Miracle's mother, it sure was strange that two ladies in a place the size of Clement's Pond would have the name Fleur.

That evening I noticed Bear sprucing up right smart, combing his hair special and brushing down his beard so it would lay flat, and even putting on his shoes instead of his regular boots. "You sure are fixing up, Bear," I told him, and he looked at me and chuckled. Fact of the matter, Bear didn't have to spruce up too much. He was right handsome any way you looked at him. I reckon he was just about the most handsome man in all of Clement's Pond.

"You going to church with us, Bear?" Aunt Ester called out, knocking on the bedroom door.

"No, Ester," Bear called back, "I reckon I'll stay at the house and see if I can't get sanctified by the young folks."

"Sanctified or starry-eyed?" Aunt Ester laughed and went on.

Looked to me like Bear didn't have to wait for the young people's meeting to get starry-eyed. The way he was acting, his eyes already had the moon and stars both in them. All during the young people's meeting I noticed how Bear couldn't stop studying Fleur Portune. When she led us in singing, he seemed to be perked up just for the sound of her voice. And when she stood up and sang "Jesus, Lover of My Soul," he acted like he was about struck dumb. I could tell he thought she was an angel, all right.

As soon as the singing was over and refreshments was announced, Bear took off follering Fleur all the way across the floor and out into the kitchen. I started off behind them, figuring if Fleur really was Miracle's mother, she might make some accidental mention of it to Bear, might start asking some questions and such about Miracle. I made myself busy near the doorway where I couldn't be seen but where I could see Bear and Fleur and hear what they was saying. I didn't want to be a sneak, but seemed like I just couldn't control myself.

Fleur was pouring cocoa into a cup when Bear walked up to her, like as if he was just wandering into the kitchen with no idea she was there. But once he was inside and close to her, he spoke right up.

"I'm Lyon's father, Bear Savage," I heard him say.

"Oh, yes," Fleur said, smiling. "I haven't lived in Clement's Pond long enough to know all the children, but I do remember Lyon. Such a polite boy."

"Where are you from, Miss Portune?" Bear asked her.

I watched Fleur's face closely. She seemed to hesitate. Then, like she was forcing it, she said, "I'm from Millerton."

So that was where she was from! Up around the northern part of the state. Maybe that was where she went back to after she left the baby at the pond, I thought. But my mind was a jumble of confusion. I had to keep reminding myself that *maybe* she wasn't Miracle's mother at all.

"Is that where your family is?" Bear asked.

"Yes," Fleur answered, looking nervous and embarrassed, like she didn't want to talk about it.

"I reckon it takes real gumption for a young woman such as yourself to leave her home and family and come to a new place."

"A woman nowadays has to have gumption, Mr. Savage. She has to be strong and look out for herself."

"I admire a woman of independence," Bear said with a smile.

Fleur smiled then, a pure and beautiful smile. "Would you like a cup of cocoa, Mr. Savage?"

"Only if you'll call me Bear."

Fleur poured the hot cocoa out of a pan on the stove into a cup for Bear. "What an unusual name. It's almost well . . . frightening."

"Protective," Bear corrected her.

"I see," Fleur said, smiling even more as she handed Bear the cup of cocoa. Then they started walking toward the door and I had to hightail it away as fast as I could. Fleur hadn't asked even one question about Miracle.

I went over to Justin and plopped down on the floor beside him. And soon as I sat down, Fulton Kramer come up and give me his ugliest snaggle-toothed grin and spouted, "If you'd got down on your knees in your closet like I told you to, temptation wouldn't of struck you, Lyon. You never would of tooken that baby. The Lord would of — "

"Why don't you mind your own business, Fulton?" Justin blasted.

Fulton glared at Justin. "You ain't exactly innocent of sin yourself, are you now? You was a part of that whole jig. You and your cotton-headed sister! The three of you is the biggest sinners that I know of in Clement's Pond right now." Fulton's grin got bigger and wider as he pointed out our mistakes.

"You're a good one to talk!" I said, and I was mad. "All you ever done in your life was smoke and drink and steal before Miss Benson come along and talked you into coming to church! The only reason you come in the first place is because you was moonin' over her!"

"You just did another sin, Lyon! Ain't you never going to learn that to *lie* is a sin?" Fulton said, and grinned again.

"You shut your mouth, Fulton! For your stupid information, we *saved* that baby from drowning in the pond!" Sylvie said, appearing suddenly and shoving her chin out toward Fulton. There was a threatening glint in her eyes that made old Fulton take a step back and close his mouth.

T-Roy Tate come up then and said, "Has the

laws found out who the mama of that baby is yet?"

"No, the laws ain't never found out!" Sylvie mocked T-Roy while giving me and Justin a secret, private look. I couldn't keep from thinking about Fleur and glancing around the room. Her and Bear was sitting by Aunt Ester's Victrola, talking to beat sixty.

"I reckon there'll be someone out here from the county anytime to take that baby," Fulton said, and I cringed at the horrible thought.

All of a sudden my feet started wobbling in my shoes and I leaned close to Justin and whispered, "Let's get out of here!" We took off with Sylvie follering us and went out on the back steps. We no sooner got out the door when Taffy appeared.

"You just go on!" Sylvie told her in a hard voice. "I, for one, ain't got nothing to say to you."

"Ain't you my best friend, Sylvie?" Taffy asked in a tiny little voice that was hardly a breath in the night air. The light from the kitchen winder fell across her face and I could see tears pop into her eyes.

"You two-faced me, Taffy!" Sylvie said in that same hard voice. Taffy raised her hands and covered her face with them and started crying. "And I thought you was my best friend! Well, I sure found you out, Taffy-two-face-Marshall! You're just like your mama! You'd do anything, even turn against your own friends, just to get one of them stupid old dolls you're always bragging about. Well, let them old dolls be your friends from now on!" Sylvie went on, and the more she said, the harder Taffy cried.

It put a pain deep inside me to see Taffy standing there with her face all covered up with her hands, crying like she could never stop.

"If Adeline can forgive us for what we done, we ought to forgive Taffy for what she done," I said, and my voice was shaking. "My daddy says there can't be a cause without an effect."

"Meaning?" Sylvie asked, giving me a sideways look.

"Meaning, if you hadn't told Taffy to begin with, Taffy couldn't of told her mama anything," I answered back right sharp.

"Lyon's right," Justin said. "You broke the promise you made to us that you wouldn't tell, Sylvie."

Sylvie wrapped her arms over her chest. I could see her staring hatefully at me from the light in the winder. "You know why I done it, Lyon," she said in a softer voice. "But I didn't mean for . . ."

She stopped. But she didn't have to say more. I knew it was her revenge for me that led her to do what she done.

"Looks to me like you want to pay me back by taking Taffy's side," she went on, raising her head.

"I'm not taking anyone's side, Sylvie," I told her.

For some time not one of us said a word. Finally Sylvie cleared her throat and said to Taffy, "If you want to be my friend again, you better never tell your mama ner no one else what

I tell you. If you do, Taffy Marshall, there's no telling what I might do."

Taffy pulled her head out of her hands and, with tears sparkling all over her cheeks, she smiled and said, "Oh, Sylvie, I won't! I swear I won't. You've been my best friend forever and ever. Don't you know how much I love you, Sylvie? Come to my house tomorrow and I'll show you all my dolls and the dresses I made and — "

"Ain't you ever going to grow up, Taffy?" Sylvie cried disgustedly. "Are you going to play with dolls and have silly play tea parties until you're ninety?"

"We can do other things," Taffy said eagerly.

Sylvie sighed. "Just don't you two-face me again, you hear?"

"Didn't I tell you I wouldn't, Sylvie?" Taffy said, but it looked to me like Zooie had already ruined Taffy for keeping things to herself. Taffy had found a way to get them dolls she loved so much out of her mama, and it looked like there wouldn't never be no secret Taffy could keep because of that.

I couldn't keep from remembering a happier time when Taffy played with them dolls and carried one or two around with her wherever she went and even talked to them, like as if they was as real to her as people was. I never could get it clear in my mind what it was about them dolls that made Taffy cling to them with such a fierce passion. She was the only girl I knowed of her age who acted that way.

"Well, I reckon we better go on inside," I said,

and I hurried past Taffy, longing in my heart to stop and put my arm around her and to make her feel better, but I went on by with my head down so I wouldn't have to look at her face.

Inside the house the first thing I seen was Bear and Fleur still sitting over by Aunt Ester's Victrola, sipping their cocoa and talking a blue streak. It looked like Bear didn't waste no time when he set his mind to getting acquainted. Next thing I knew, he was saying he was going to take Aunt Ester's Chevy, soon as she got in from church, and run Fleur into town to her house. It sure beat all I ever seen, how quick Bear took to Fleur Portune!

After everyone went home and I was in bed, Skeeter come into my room and jumped up on the bed. "I liked it tonight, Lyon," he said. "We ain't had no party like this since my ma went to heaven."

"You stay in Clement's Pond long enough and you'll get your fill of parties. Leastways, church kind. Nothing much to do around here but go to church and such. You got to go to Tylersville to see shows and things," I told him. "Hey, where was your daddy tonight?"

"He be looking for some rooms for us to stay. He says we can't live off Miss Ester for the rest of our lives," Skeeter answered.

"Your daddy got a job already?"

"Uh-huh. And if we can get some rooms, he can start work tomorry."

"Maybe he should ask Miss Adeline, Skeeter. She's got a nice little house and a real soft spot in her heart for kids."

Skeeter frowned. "My daddy said Miss Addie do have a pure and kind heart but he won't even go to see Miss Addie."

"I reckon I know why," I said with a yawn.

Hardly a day went by that Bear wasn't over to Fleur's place and it wasn't even a month before Aunt Ester started saying, "There's something brewing up between Bear and that singing teacher, and it ain't a pot of sassafras tea!"

"What you reckon is brewing up, Aunt Ester?" I asked, and Aunt Ester smiled.

"Boy, there's many a thing can brew up twixt a man and a woman. You'll understand what I mean by and by."

On a Saturday night not long after Bear took up good and strong with Fleur, he put on his best pants and shirt and started brushing down his beard and told me to get all gussied up too.

"How come, Bear?" I asked him, but I had a hunch why.

"We've been invited to supper with Miss Fleur at her house," Bear answered.

"*Both* of us?"

"Yep. Both," Bear said, and when I saw him putting on his only necktie, I knew there was bound to be more than just supper on his mind.

21
I Get an Earful

The sign outside Fleur's house said:

VOICE LESSONS BY THE HOUR
MISS FLEUR PORTUNE — TEACHER

Bear lifted his shoe and rubbed it against the back of his pant leg to polish it and knocked on the door. Fleur come right away with a pretty smile and friendly greeting and told us to come in.

"I ain't never had stuffed peppers before," I told her when she asked me if I liked them. The only thing Aunt Ester ever stuffed was a turkey at Thanksgiving and sometimes chickens in between.

"You're in for a big treat," Bear said with a grin, like he'd already had the experience of them stuffed peppers. "Next to your Aunt Ester, Fleur is the best cook this side of heaven."

Fleur's face turned all pink and she smiled

and blinked her eyes at Bear, like as if she was
real shy, except she wasn't. There was something up. I could tell that. Bear didn't get all
gussied up for nothing and Fleur didn't invite
no kid like me for stuffed peppers for nothing.
And she didn't stand there and blush for
nothing, neither. Like Aunt Ester said, whatever was brewing, it sure wasn't a pot of sassafras tea!

When we set down at the table, I felt plumb
embarrassed because of the beautiful lace tablecloth and shiny plates and glasses. Fleur had
even put lace-edged napkins beside our plates.
Aunt Ester's dishes most always had a little
chip or a crack in them. I ate so much I felt like
I was being rude, but Fleur said to never mind,
to eat all I wanted and then some. So I did. After
a while I got drowsy from all that food so Fleur
told me to go lay down on the divan and rest.
While I was resting, I closed my eyes and I
guess Bear and Fleur thought I fell asleep
because, the next thing I knew, Fleur was saying in a strained voice, "There is something I
must tell you, Bear . . ."

And she commenced to tell the whole story
about leaving Miracle at the pond. I didn't have
to see Bear's face to know he was shocked. I
could tell it from the tone of his voice.

"How could you have even thought of leaving
your little baby like that, Fleur?"

Fleur sniffled and sounded like she was
getting ready to cry.

"I . . . I did it because . . . because I was going
to kill myself, Bear! You see, my baby's father

had run off and my family threw me out of the house, told me I was no good and never would be with an . . . an illegitimate baby on my hands. They . . . they threw us both out just like they'd throw out an unwanted stranger. . . ." Fleur went on and had to stop again. "I didn't see how an outcast like me could ever do any good for a tiny, helpless baby."

"Your family was wrong, Fleur. Bad wrong to do that to you," Bear said in a low, husky voice.

"Oh, Bear, they called my son horrible names! Names I could never repeat in a million years! They said he would be as no account as me! That I'd brought shame on them that could never be erased . . ."

"There, there, Fleur," Bear said with sympathy, and I knew he was pulling Fleur into his arms. I didn't have to open my eyes to know that. "There ain't no baby born that deserves a bad-name-calling. It's your family who has brought shame on themselves for what they done to you . . ." Bear stopped like he was thinking hard. Then he went on, "Fleur, why didn't you go back to make sure the baby was all right?" There was pure emotion in his voice. "To leave him at the pond . . ."

"I did go back, Bear! I went back that very night, the very hour! It had started to rain and I made my cousin drive back. I'd decided that maybe, somehow, I could keep him, that things would work out, that I could get a job and hire someone to care for him. But . . . but he was gone!

"Oh, the nightmare I went through! I ran all around that pond with the rain soaking into my skin, looking in every place. When I couldn't find him, I started to throw myself into the pond, but my cousin grabbed me and forced me back into the car and refused to let me go on searching. He'd been to the pond many, many times fishing and told me that the baby just had to have been found by someone. And, as it turned out, thank God, that's exactly what happened."

Fleur stopped and Bear started saying, "There, there," again and I reckoned he was plumb mellered out with sympathy. Fleur soon got her voice back and said, "I . . . I was too ill to work and support myself. After I left my son, all I could do was go back home. No one, not even Mama, asked about the baby. It seemed like they didn't care what happened to him as long as he was out of their lives.

"But as soon as I got my strength back and made some money, I came back here to look for my son. Somehow, I knew I'd find him. When I heard about Adeline Newberry having him, it was the first moment I could breathe, Bear. Oh, I was so grateful. I've wanted so much to thank Lyon and Justin and Sylvie for finding my baby, but how could I let them know I was Miracle's mother?"

"I understand, Fleur," Bear said in his kindest voice.

"Oh, Bear, how am I ever going to tell Adeline Newberry that her 'miracle baby' is my own son that I abandoned?"

"The question is, are you ready now to tell her, Fleur?" Bear asked.

"Yes! Yes! But what are she and everyone in Clement's Pond going to think? What will the police do?"

"It don't matter what folks think," Bear said firmly. "As for the police, we'll face that together . . . when the time comes."

I popped one eye open and looked through the shadow of my eyelashes at Bear and Fleur. His arms was still around her and she was sniffling against his chest.

"Wh-what d-do you m-mean, Bear?" she asked through her sniffles.

"I mean, I want to marry you, Fleur Portune," Bear answered. "I want to make you my wife."

Both my eyes sprang open wide!

"But . . . oh, Bear, I can't . . . can't be married now!"

"Now, what do *you* mean, gal?"

"Don't you know that everyone would talk even more than they are going to when they find out Adeline's baby is really . . . really *my* baby?"

I had a throat full of lumps and I felt like I was going to choke! It was all I could do to keep laying there on that divan pretending I was sawing logs!

"You let me worry about that," Bear said sternly.

"You don't understand, Bear! Listen to me! When a woman marries for the first time, tradition says she must be wed in . . . wed in white. Don't you see, you sweet, kind, good man? I can't . . . can't ever wear a gown of white!"

Bear suddenly threw his head back and exploded with a wild "Geeeehaaaa!"

"Why are you laughing at me, Bear Savage?" Fleur asked, looking horrified.

"Why, gal, you're as pure and white as any woman walking in this town! You don't need a gown of white to prove nothing to a soul! Besides, *I'm* the one who's wanting to marry you, not the whole of Clement's Pond! If it's white you'll be wanting to be wed in, then by geebers, you'll have it and the town be hanged."

Fleur started crying in a great rush of tears then and ran back into Bear's arms, saying, "Oh, Bear . . . how can you live and be so wonderful? Oh, I love you! I love you!"

Bear soothed Fleur with a lot of soft words that I couldn't make out because his voice was all caught in her hair. But after a few minutes he pulled his face away and said in a deep and serious voice, "What we got to do now is go to Adeline and tell her the truth."

"Oh, I'm so afraid of what this will do to her, Bear," Fleur said.

"From all appearances, Adeline is a mighty strong woman. I doubt anything can set her back too much," Bear tried to assure Fleur. And he added, "We'd better wake up that sleeping boy of mine and tell him he's going to have a new mama before too much longer."

I shut my eyes real quick. I sure didn't want Bear to think I'd been listening to every word him and Fleur said. My heart was pounding to beat sixty, I was so excited. Fleur Portune. . . my new mama. I sure never expected that. Not in a quintillion years! But it come into my mind all of a sudden that if Bear married Fleur, they might not stay in Clement's Pond. They might take Miracle and leave!

Seemed like I just got Bear back for my own and would be losing him again. Maybe for good this time.

22
Bear Breaks the News

When we left Fleur's house, I walked straight out to the Chevy like as if I had been sleeping all night and got in, pretending not to notice that Bear had lingered behind to give Fleur a hug and a kiss.

When we was on the road on our way back to Aunt Ester's, Bear asked, "You woke up good, boy?"

"Yes, sir," I told him.

"Good. I've got some news for you, son. News that may surprise you."

"What is it, Bear?" I had to ask it so's Bear wouldn't suspect I already knew what he was going to tell me.

"Me and Miss Fleur are planning on getting married." Bear took his eyes off the road, turned, and looked at me.

"For sure and for certain?" I asked, trying to sound just as surprised as I figured Bear expected me to be.

"For sure and for certain." He looked back at the road. "How do you feel about that, Lyon?"

Did Bear want the truth? I wondered. Did he want to hear how I'd rather him not marry Fleur Portune and how I'd of rather him and me live together at Aunt Ester's all the rest of our lives and go fishing and hunting and doing things together with no one around to bother us? Or would he rather hear polite words? I looked at his strong profile with his beard jutting down into the front of his collar and his eyes looking straight ahead at the road and I swallered hard, wishing, as pretty as Fleur Portune was, she didn't have to come between us.

"Well, boy?"

I cleared my throat. "Well ... well, Bear, I'm right pleased, I reckon," I said, and I watched a big grin spread across Bear's face. I'd said the right thing all right.

When we got home Aunt Ester was still up, sitting in the front room in her rocking chair reading her Bible. I figured Bear was going to tell her about him and Fleur planning to get hitched, so I headed straight to the bedroom. After I got in bed, I could hear them talking in low voices, but not so low that the sound didn't come right through the walls.

"Bear, are you sure this is what you want?" I heard Aunt Ester ask, and Bear answered right up, "There's not a doubt in my mind, Ester."

"Well, in that case, I'd be mighty proud iffen you and Fleur would be married here in our house. We could have a nice ceremony with the preacher and a cake and friends and . . ."

For a minute Bear didn't say anything. Then I heard him say, "I'm not so sure about the friends, Ester." I knew he was worrying about going to see Adeline and the town finding out about Miracle. "But I'd be proud to be married here. And I thank you for the offer." He most likely knew Aunt Ester would forgive Fleur when she found out.

"Well, of course there'll be friends come, Bear," Aunt Ester said. She sounded like her dander was up just thinking about folks giving Bear a turndown at his own wedding, though after Bear come to bed and was snoring to beat sixty, I laid awake wondering if anyone would show up for the wedding. If folks found out about Fleur and Miracle, like as not we'd all get mighty lonesome for company.

"You'd better get a move on, Lyon, and get yourself over to Adeline's and pick them apples for her so she'll have a-plenty for her apple pies. We don't want to short no one at the church social on Adeline's apple pies," Aunt Ester told me at the breakfast table.

"Yes, ma'am," I said, hurrying up over my fried egg.

"May as well go to Adeline's with me and Fleur, son," Bear said as he pushed back his chair from the table and stood up.

Aunt Ester looked up over her glasses at Bear. "You and Fleur going to Adeline's, Bear?" she asked in a curious way.

"I reckon so, Ester," Bear told her, and he patted me on my shoulder as he walked out of the kitchen. I could see he'd left a curious look on Uncle Clayborn's face too. But neither one of them said anything as I got up from the table, pushed my chair in, and follered Bear out of the room.

Course I knew why Bear and Fleur was going to Adeline's. Didn't take much to figure that out. I'd just wondered how long it was going to take them. I'd wondered, too, just how long after that it was going to be before Bear and Fleur got hitched up. So far, I hadn't heard any more about it except that I was right: Bear had been hinting at not staying in Clement's Pond.

Well, I had my satchel all ready to go! I'd stuffed it with everything I owned just about, except my clothes, and I'd saved out my mama's picture to put in last. I didn't know where we would be going, and Bear hadn't said nothing about me going too, but wasn't no way I'd ever let Bear out of my sight again!

We went in Aunt Ester's Chevy to pick up Fleur at her house, then drove to Adeline's house. Fleur was as pretty and as smiling as you please and I studied her right smart as we rode along in the car. She might be marrying my daddy, but she'd never shake loose of me!

When we went up the steps of Adeline's porch, we heard Adeline call out from inside the house, "Who is it?"

But before we could answer, she was at the door with Miracle in her arms. The minute she seen who was on the porch she come out the door and said warmly, "I'm so glad to see you, Miss Portune. And you too, Bear. What a nice surprise."

"Good afternoon, Adeline," Bear said, and my eyes shot to Fleur. I knew she must be trembling all over from just looking at her own little baby in Adeline Newberry's arms. "Looks like you got your hands full," Bear went on with a chuckle.

Adeline smiled a real big smile and said, "And it's a pure joy, I declare, Bear."

Bear sort of cleared his throat then and said, "Me and Miss Fleur here come to have a little chat with you, Adeline."

"Well, come right in, please," Adeline said, and she pulled open the screen door and allowed Fleur to walk into the house first. I studied Fleur's face real close as she passed Miracle and I saw her give him what Aunt Ester would call "a most desirous and longing look," like as if she wanted to reach out and grab that little baby right out of Adeline's arms. But she didn't make a move toward him. She just passed on by with a smile for Adeline that looked like she'd cut it out of a face in the Sears and Roebuck catalog and pasted it on.

I was ready to march right in the door after Adeline, but Bear reached out and tapped my head with his knuckles and said to Adeline, "I brought my apple picker with me."

Adeline smiled. "Thank you for coming, Lyon. I'll have a nice cool glass of lemonade waiting for you when you're all finished."

It was for sure and for certain them grown-ups wanted me out of the way so they could talk, even if I did come on a purpose of picking them apples. I went around the side of the house where three big apple trees stood chock-full of big red juicy-looking apples and climbed up in the closest one to the house. From the limb I was on, I could practically see right into Adeline's front-room winder. I couldn't see no movement, though, because the sun was shining on the glass and making a sharp cut across my eyes. I blinked and looked away. Curiosity didn't do a feller no good when he was stuck up in a tree shaking apples out of it.

"What you doing up there?" a voice called from the front of the yard. I looked down through the leafy branches and saw Taffy leaning against Adeline's fence. But I went on looking for apples, like as if I didn't even know she was around, and out of pure nervousness, I yelled "Timberrrrrrr..." as I shook one of the branches and about a dozen apples bombed the ground below. Next time I looked, Taffy was under the tree, leaning against the trunk, looking straight up at me and smiling.

"What's the matter, Lyon? There an old cat up there that's runned away with your tongue?" Taffy giggled and I could of fell right out of that tree, it sounded so pure and cute.

Taffy looked so pretty in a pink sweater, and with her dark braid thrown across her shoulder and her mouth parted in a sweet smile, it near about made my heart thunder right out of my chest just to look at her. Seemed like our eyes was attached until an apple tumbled down through the tree and hit Taffy on her arm.

"Taffy! Are you hurt?" My heart started thumping even harder then. Taffy's lip curled up and for a second it looked like she was going to cry. "Are you all right, Taffy?"

She rubbed her arm and said, "Well, I reckon as to how I better get away from here before you kill me, Lyon Savage!" She walked away, but she hadn't even reached Adeline's porch when we both were stopped stone-still by an awful sound.

"Oh, Lord, tell me it ain't true! Oh, blessed Jesus, no!"

Taffy turned and our eyes met, then we both stared at the house. For sure and for certain, those loud, hurtful words had come right out of Adeline Newberry's mouth! I gulped and shoved a branch out of the way to stare across at the winder, but the sun was still in the glass, making it too hard for me to see inside. I looked back down at Taffy. She was still standing there looking up at me, a deep, puzzled expression on her face.

Next thing we heard was muffled voices rising and falling like the winds that come in autumn and bluster for a while, then fade away, then come back again even stronger. No doubt about it, there was a storm brewing in that house and it carried the mood of thunder and lightning with it. Every now and then Bear's voice come like it had a soothing pitch to it, but I couldn't make out what he was saying. And every now and then, another burst of crying would shatter the air between the house and the apple trees. I gulped again, knowing in my heart what was taking place inside Adeline's front room.

"Lyon, what you reckon is going on in there?" Taffy asked with her eyes big and her voice low.

But before I could say a word, Adeline's voice rang out again. "Oh Lord, help me to accept this . . . Fleur Portune has come to claim her own baby!" My eyes flew back to the winder, but I still couldn't see anything. Then there was crying like I never heard in my life, flying out through them words, and it sure took a lot of deep and heavy breathing to keep from crying myself. I reckoned it was near about to kill Adeline to find out that Miracle had a true mama after all, and she'd come to claim him.

When I looked back down at Taffy, she was gazing up at me with her mouth dropped open and a shocked expression on her face. Suddenly she flipped around and started running across the yard.

"Taffy! Come back!" I yelled after her, but she didn't stop running, not even once, after she slung open the gate and took off out it. I didn't have to wonder where Taffy was running to so fast. I was certain she was on her way home to tell her mama everything she'd heard. Taffy had made a promise, but it didn't look like she was going to keep it.

I started climbing down so fast I nearly fell, but before I could get down she'd already disappeared. I sighed a deep sigh and leaned my head into the leaves against a limb and closed my eyes, but I could still see Taffy with her skirt flying, running off to tell Zooie what all she'd heard. Soon as Zooie got the word, it would take no time for the news to be all over Clement's Pond.

"I never wanted to hurt you, Miss Adeline . . . oh, please believe me . . ." It was Fleur's voice, trembling out of the doorway. Then Bear's voice come again, soothing and low, then there was crying again. It sounded like Adeline and Fleur was crying together and pretty soon Miracle commenced to cry. But then something amazing happened; it seemed like all the crying started changing to laughter.

It sure was a mystery to me how folks could carry on so. Next thing I knew, they was all three, including Miracle in Fleur's arms, coming out on the front porch and Fleur was saying, "Thank you, Miss Adeline, from the bottom of my heart, for all you've done. I'll be forever grateful to you." Her face was streaked with tears, but she was still as pretty as could be.

"I wondered how long it would be before Miracle's mother would come." Adeline spoke up and her chin was quivering so bad, I didn't see how she could even talk. "I must have known in my heart of hearts that the Lord was only letting me keep this precious child until you could get your life arranged and come for him." Adeline put her arm around Fleur then. "The Lord works in wondrous ways to bring folks together," she said.

Bear leaned over then and put a kiss on Adeline's wet cheek and Fleur did the same and

I reckon one of the leaves pierced me in my eyes, because, next thing I knew, they were stinging something fearful. I had to sniff hard to make the tears stay back.

Bear must have heard my sniff. He turned and looked up at me and called out, "You got them apples ready for Miss Adeline, boy?"

"Yes, sir!" I called back, and I grabbed the closest limb and started shaking it like a fury.

23
A Conniver
and a Stinking Old Goat

Two days later me and Justin and Sylvie met on the road walking to the school bus and the first thing Sylvie said when she seen me was, "Lyon, have you heard what folks is saying?"

"What are they saying?" I wasn't sure I wanted to know.

"They're saying Fleur Portune is Miracle's mother and that your father is going to marry her. I wouldn't have to think twice to know who started that talk," Sylvie said, smacking her lips.

"It was Taffy, all right," I said out of the pure bitterness in me.

"And Zooie."

"It would of come out anyway," Justin said. "Everyone was bound to find out that Fleur is Miracle's mother, sooner or later."

I snorted to myself. Sure. But Taffy had to be

the one. A pain rose up inside me just thinking about it.

We reached the bus stop and waited in the chilly morning air for the bus to come. While we stood there, all scrunched up in our old thin coats that had seen more winters on other kids' backs than our own, we seen Taffy come swinging down the road carrying her lunch sack.

"Look at her! Thinks she's something, don't she? I'll bet she got two old dolls, instead of one, for *that* juicy information!"

"Hi, y'all guys," Taffy said with a smile of innocence on her face when she reached us. No one spoke. She frowned, staring at us in a hard and puzzled way. "What's wrong?" she asked.

"As if you didn't know!" Sylvie snapped.

"Aw, don't be so hard on her," Justin said, scraping his brogan across the dirt.

Taffy's eyes was as big as the eyes of an old mama cat. I couldn't tell if she was surprised or askeered.

"What kind of doll did your mama promise you this time, Taffy?" Sylvie asked with a spiteful sneer. "Is it one of them fancy dressed ones from Paris, France, or is it one of them old cheap, plain ones from the Sears and Roebuck catalog?"

"None of my dolls is cheap and plain, Sylvie!" Taffy cried. "All my dolls is fancy and beautiful! More beautiful than anything in life!" Tears sprang into Taffy's eyes and mad as I was at her, I had to look down to keep from wanting to rush to her and put my arm around her.

Seemed like, all of a sudden, I realized why

Taffy needed them dolls. It was because she didn't have no family to love. *Them dolls was her family.* It looked like they was all she had to hold on to and to love. Trouble was, I didn't see how they could love her back. Even now after I was sure of what she'd done, I still felt sorry for her and wished I could give her comfort. But I knew if I even tried and Zooie found out, she'd skin me alive.

"You're a conniver and a stinking old goat!" Sylvie spit. "Miss Fleur never done nothing to you except be nice to you and teach you them songs!"

I looked up and Taffy seemed to shrink before my eyes. The green-and-brown-plaid coat she was wearing suddenly seemed to swaller her and all I could see was her dark head popping over the top of the collar.

"Sylvie, why are you talking to me like this? Ain't you still my friend?" Taffy asked in a trembly little voice.

All at once Sylvie lunged toward Taffy and pushed her shoulder hard, making Taffy stumble back. "Stop it!" me and Justin shouted at the same time. But Sylvie took another step toward Taffy and grabbed her braid and started twisting it. Taffy pulled back, screaming. Me and Justin shouted again and Justin grabbed hold of Sylvie's hand and yanked it away from Taffy's braid. Sylvie glared at Justin, then at me.

"Y'all guys are on *her* side, ain't you?" she cried. "Ain't you got no feeling for your soon-to-be-stepmama, Lyon?" she blasted at me. "Don't you care what folks is saying?"

"I got feeling! Plenty of feeling! I got more feeling than you know! But you ain't going to pick on Taffy!" I blasted back. "Her mama picks on her enough!"

"I knew it!" Sylvie cried with a look of horror on her face. "I knew you loved Taffy! That's why you stick up for her all the time!"

The school bus rumbled up then and drowned out the rest of what Sylvie was saying. But I knew Justin's eyes was on me and that he was thinking about what Sylvie had said. We got on the bus and for the first time, Sylvie and Taffy didn't sit together.

"Is what Sylvie said true, Lyon?" Justin asked me as the bus took off.

"Is what true?" I asked him, but I knew what he meant, all right.

"About you loving Taffy." There was a funny look on Justin's face.

"No. No, it ain't true," I said, chomping down hard on my words.

"That's good," Justin said like he was relieved. "Because it's always going to be you and Sylvie, and Taffy and me."

I stared at Justin, not knowing what to say.

"My mama says Taffy has got a weakness in her that needs to be made strong," Justin went on, sounding like as if *he* was the one could make her strong.

I crossed my arms over my chest and sunk down into the seat and stared out the winder.

The fields and big trees and old barns passed before my eyes, but I could hardly see them for all the thoughts crowding before my vision. Justin was my best friend but if I was going to spend any "always" with Sylvie, I was glad I'd packed my bags to leave with Bear and Fleur. When we reached the school and got off the bus, Taffy come running up to me and said, "I don't see no reason for Sylvie to get so mad at me, Lyon. Why was she saying all them things and jumping on me like she done?"

I stared at Taffy, wishing she was as sweet and innocent as she appeared. "I reckon you're just a little conniver, like Sylvie said," I told her.

"That ain't true, Lyon!"

"You went straight home from Adeline's that day and told your mama every word you heard!"

Taffy stopped and grabbed my arm. "No, Lyon! I swear before God, and he can strike me dead if I'm lying to you. I didn't tell mama ner no one nothing I heard that day at Adeline's! I ain't never, ever going to tell Mama a thing again!" I pulled my arm away and started walking real fast with Taffy running alongside me, trying to keep up. "I swear it, Lyon! Do you know why, Lyon? Lyon, do you know why?"

"*Why*?" I asked grudgingly.

"Because . . . because I seen hurt in your eyes when you knew I told about what you and Sylvie and Justin done. That's why." I turned and stared at her. "All's I want is for you to believe me, Lyon. Say you do, Lyon. Please. Sylvie don't like me no more and I ain't got no other friends . . ."

I stopped and looked into Taffy's face. It was fierce with desperation. Her eyes was full of tears and, for a reason I couldn't understand, I wanted to kiss her pink lips and never stop.

"Lyon," she said softly, "please, Lyon . . . please believe me!"

"Go on and get away from me, Taffy!" I yelled, and I started running across the school-yard to get away from her. I couldn't stand being so close to her and hearing her tiny little pleading voice and seeing her shining dark eyes and soft lips. Feelings sprang up inside me that I didn't want to leap out. So I ran.

24
Bad News Travels Fast

News about Fleur being Miracle's mama traveled up and down every road in Clement's Pond faster than a jack-rabbit can run. There wasn't a corner to crawl into ner a hole to crawl out of where someone wasn't gossiping about it. Folks was saying all manner of things against Fleur. Things I wouldn't even want to repeat. When they found out Bear was about to marry her, it just made matters worse.

"Bad news always travels faster than good news," Uncle Clayborn stated as a matter of fact one afternoon.

I was setting the table in the kitchen for Aunt Ester when she blasted out with, "Looks like I was just born to have to defend folks! If it ain't one, it's another!" When she had found out about Fleur being Miracle's mother, all she'd said was, "If Adeline can forgive her, I don't have no trouble."

"You ought to of been one of them high-toned

eeturnies like they got over to Tylersville, Ester," Uncle Clayborn chuckled as his hand shot out toward the platter of pork chops.

Aunt Ester reached out and slapped the back of his hand. "Leave it be, Clayborn! Give the boy a chance to get the utensils on the table!"

"Aw, flitter, Essie!" Uncle Clayborn grumbled, pulling up his chair and sitting down in it.

Aunt Ester went to the stove and took the mashed pertaters out of a pot and put them in a bowl. "Be sure you set a place for Ferdie, Lyon. He'll be coming by to pick up him and the young'uns' belongings. I reckon he'll be wanting to have a bite to eat before he goes."

More than a bite, I thought as I got another plate for Ferdie. He hadn't walked away from a meal since coming back to Clement's Pond, that I knew of.

"He got him a place?" Uncle Clayborn asked.

"He's got him and the boys a fine big room in Sanders' boardinghouse," Aunt Ester answered.

"Too bad he's too stubborn to see Adeline," Uncle Clayborn said, reaching for a pork chop again. This time Aunt Ester let him.

I dropped the last fork down by Clayborn's plate and plopped down in my chair. Aunt Ester sat down and sighed. "Well, I reckon there ain't no need to count on many for Bear's wedding. From the looks of things, there'll be mighty few here to congratulate him and his bride."

"Folks will forget—" Uncle Clayborn started, and Aunt Ester cut him off with, "Forget! They ain't even had time to digest it good yet!"

I looked down at my plate, feeling bitterness

fill up in me for Taffy. I could just see her and her new dolls and Zooie's tongue flapping all over town like a flag in the wind.

Aunt Ester sighed again. "What Fleur Portune needs is some good Christian understanding. If she didn't have Bear to stand up for her, folks would go to preaching on the street corners about what a wicked and cruel woman she is!"

"Miss Fleur sure don't seem cruel and wicked," I spoke up.

Aunt Ester reached over and touched my hand. "And she ain't neither, boy. Sometimes circumstances come along in life that would shiver the timbers of the strongest soul. Things get so bad, a feller just don't know what to do, and sometimes he does the worst possible thing he can do."

"Is that what Fleur done, Aunt Ester?"

"Yes, boy, that's what she done."

"I sure do hate it that Taffy told her mama what she heard at Adeline's," I said, glaring at the wall and wishing I could really hate Taffy for causing trouble again. "If she hadn't told Zooie . . ."

"Why, boy, where did you get a notion like that?" Aunt Ester asked, and I looked at her. "Far as I know, Taffy didn't tell Zooie a thing about Fleur. Fact of the matter is, it was Vi, over to the hat shop, who told Zooie one day when she went in to have a hat made."

All at once I turned hot, like my whole insides was boiling over and ready to bubble out my skin! I felt so sick I wanted to throw up! "It . . .

it was?" I could hardly get the words out, I felt so rotten.

"And it was Trudence Welch who told Vi," Aunt Ester went on. "And Emma Tallsworthy was the one who told Trudence. Don't rightly know who told Emma. Boy, you look plumb sick! Pass the biscuits, Clayborn."

"Eat up, boy," Uncle Clayborn said, passing the plate of biscuits to Aunt Ester. "Worse'll come to worst, then it'll get better. You'll see. Besides, whatever is to come, Bear will meet it head-on."

"Maybe the boy wants to wait on Ferdie," Aunt Ester said.

"He's taking a chance, if he waits for him," Uncle Clayborn chuckled, licking the pork-chop grease off his fingers.

"What is it, boy?" Aunt Ester asked, looking at me with a frown of concern on her face. "You fretting about Bear and Fleur not having a nice wedding? Well, if that's what's on your mind, don't let it bother you. We'll have a fine wedding and, if no one comes, we'll have all the more cake to eat."

"I'll vote for that," Uncle Clayborn said.

I jumped out of my chair before I even knew I was going to do it and flew out of the house and around to the back and didn't stop until I'd reached Miss Pitty-Pat. She turned and give me a look, like as if to ask: What had I done now that was so bad? I rested my cheek against her old hairy one and whispered, "I've wronged Taffy, Miss Pitty-Pat. I've wronged her bad and I reckon she won't never forget it. And on top of that, Aunt Ester's house will be empty on Bear's wedding day. I reckon there won't be a soul to come and wish my daddy well." I could feel my tears soaking into Miss Pitty-Pat's musty, hairy cheek. I sniffed hard and said with a shudder, "Well, I don't give a durn! If folks we've knowed all our lives want to treat us like strangers, let them! Durn their old hides, anyway! Let them!"

When I walked around to the front of the house, Bear was standing there, leaning on the fencepost, like as if he'd been waiting for me. He smiled when he saw me and when I got near he reached out and pulled me up close to him. Seemed like I hadn't seen him for a week.

"Lyon, I know you been feeling neglected, son, but there's so much going on right now . . ."

"You been helping Fleur, Bear," I spoke up.

"That I have, boy. You know, after the wedding, we got a serious matter coming up. Me and Fleur will have to go over to Tylersville to talk to the district attorney about . . . about what happened with the baby and all. Fleur might even get a criminal charge against her and there is the possibility she won't get Miracle back. In case that does happen, we're praying mighty hard that Adeline will get to keep him. The thing is, we all got to keep our hopes up."

"Yes, sir," I said. "I sure will do that."

"There's something else I been meaning to talk to you about, son. If the worst thing happens and Fleur is sent away somewhere, I'll be wanting to be as close to wherever she is as I can be." I reckon what I'd been thinking was about to come true. Bear would be leaving Clement's Pond. "But it don't mean I've forgot about you and it don't change things between you and me. And what I want you to know, Lyon, is where I go, you go." Bear stopped and looked down. "Your home is with me and Fleur."

"Yes, sir," I said, and I couldn't hold back the grin that broke out across my face.

"I know you couldn't help knowing my feelings, son, but I just wanted to put them into words," Bear went on.

After all that had happened, I reckoned I was ready to leave Clement's Pond.

That night I went through my satchel just to make sure I had my pocketknife that Uncle Clayborn give me and the colored rocks that come from the bottom of the pond and the gold bracelet that had belonged to my mama that Aunt Ester give to me one Christmas. I'd had all these things a mighty long time and I sure didn't aim to leave them behind when I left Clement's Pond.

25
The Tragic End
of Taffy's Dolls

It sure was a day made for a wedding, I thought as I strolled down into the pasture where Miss Pitty-Pat stood. She was standing there just like always, with her head turned away, ignoring me. But she knew I was coming, all right. She always knew when I was on my way to talk to her.

"Well, Miss Pitty-Pat," I said as I put my arms around her neck and pressed my face against her cheek, "looks like I'm going to get me a stepmama today. Looks like the Lord put that old sun up in the sky and pushed the clouds back just so Bear and Fleur could have themselves a beautiful day to get hitched on." Miss Pitty-Pat nodded her head up and down just like she understood exactly what I was saying.

"Lyyyyooonnn!" It was Aunt Ester calling for me. Looked like I never could get away from her for long. "Lyyyyooonnn!"

I give Miss Pitty-Pat a tight squeeze around

her neck and kissed her old hairy cheek and she turned her head away, like as if it didn't mean a thing to her. But I knew it did. I reckon all that old mare lived for was the attention I give her.

Up at the house Aunt Ester said, "Take this here basket and go down by the pond and find some pretty wildflowers for the table. A fancy tablecloth and fine borried dishes ain't presentable without a flower centerpiece." She shoved the basket into my belly. "Go on, now, Pick all you can find and don't take all day iffen you want to see your daddy say his marriage vows."

I hurried out on the road and started running with the basket in my hand. The whole road was peaceful and still. There wasn't a sound nowhere . . . except until I got close to Taffy's house. I slowed down to a walk when I neared her gate, and what I heard made a cold chill near about freeze my innards. It was Taffy screaming! At first I wanted to run on by, to pretend to myself that I didn't hear a thing. If I could just start running again . . . but it was like as if I was trapped right there. Seemed like, if there was a commotion around, fate was determined to sling me right into it! Taffy's screams got louder and I knew I couldn't just go on and ignore them. I ran to the gate, dropped the basket, and plunged into the yard. Near the house, I slunk along a winder and heard Zooie shout savagely, "That ought to learn you, you ungrateful little fool!"

Taffy screamed again and something made a loud, dull thud of a sound. I pressed my ear to the wall of the house and heard Taffy scream out, "No, Mama! Mama, no! Oh, please, Mama!"

"You and them old dolls! You're as useless as them old dolls is!" Another loud thud and Taffy cried out like as if her heart was being ripped right out of her. "I ain't never going to spend good grocery money on them old dolls again!"

Then there was a terrible noise that I knew could only be a slap splitting across Taffy's face from Zooie's mean hand. I wanted to rush into that house and shove Zooie out of the way and take Taffy off somewhere where her mama could never mistreat her again, and I started for the gate when Zooie come storming out the front door. She crossed the porch and yard, and headed down the road like as if she was filled with the wrath of God, like her legs had a motor in them, making them go. Her head was all bent forward and her arms was swinging up and down. I never saw any woman move so quick. I rushed up on the porch and pulled the door open. The first thing I seen was Taffy sitting on the floor surrounded by all her beloved dolls that was torn half to bits. Tears was streaming down her cheeks like a running stream and she was trying to shove one of the dolls' heads back into its neck.

"Taffy," I said, and she looked up.

"Look what she done, Lyon," Taffy cried, holding up the headless doll's body. "Look what my mama done to my dolls!" And she went back to crying.

I went inside and sat down on the floor beside Taffy. "Why did your mama do this, Taffy?"

Taffy sniffled back her tears and whimpered, "Because . . . because she's in a wild mood about your d-daddy marrying Fleur, Lyon. I could feel it brewing from the minute she heard about it. And today . . . well, it being Bear's wedding day . . ."

"But why would your mama beat you and destroy your dolls just because of Bear marrying Fleur?"

Taffy sniffed again and stared at me. "Don't you know my mama has loved Bear for years and years, Lyon? Don't you know if she could stop that wedding, she would?" She looked around the floor at all her dolls ripped and torn and banged to pieces. Even their beautiful golden and dark hair was ripped out of their heads and their dresses torn away from them. It looked so awful, my heart near about broke for Taffy sitting there crying and looking like her world had come to an end. Them dolls looked as dead as Taffy must have wanted to be.

"I didn't tell Mama nothing, Lyon. I kept my promise. I wish you believed me," Taffy said, looking up at me. Her eyes was so shiny from tears it was hard to tell their true color. "I didn't tell her, not even to get a new doll for my collection."

"I know you didn't tell, Taffy. And I'm proud you didn't," I told her gently, and I reached out and put my hand on her shoulder. Soon as I did it, I wished I could move closer to her and comfort her. We stared at each other and something in her eyes told me she'd let me come closer, but I was too askeered.

Suddenly she looked nervous and picked up one of the dolls and fidgeted with the strings of hair that was left on its head. "You'd better go, Lyon. There's no telling what Mama might do if she comes back and finds you in the house."

I had an idea. "Maybe I can fix these dolls for you, Taffy," I told her, picking up one of the bodies without an arm and head.

"Do you think you could, Lyon? Oh, do you think you could?" Her face brightened.

"Tell you what, you get them all put in a sack and bring them down to Aunt Ester's when you get the chance, and I'll try." I stood up and looked down at Taffy. If I was older and could of, I would of tooken her away right then. I would of bought her a hundred dolls! A million! All she wanted. "I sure hope you'll be okay, Taffy," I said, stopping at the door. "If you ain't . . . well, I reckon Aunt Ester could make a pallet on the floor for you. She ain't turned away no one yet."

"Why, Lyon," Taffy said with a surprised look on her face, just like as if Zooie had never laid a hand on her, "I wouldn't leave my mama! I couldn't do that!"

I stared at Taffy. How could she feel that way, I wondered, after what her mama had done to her and to them dolls she loved so much? I didn't understand how she could still feel anything for Zooie, mean as she was. I wondered if having a mama like Zooie was better than having no mama at all.

I hurried out the door then and picked up the basket at the gate, feeling less like picking flowers than anything I could think of, and went on down the road. Near the pond I found a lot of white daisies and dandelions and stuck them in the basket. I pulled up some mustard grass for color and two bright flowers I found growing all by themselves. I even pulled up some four-leaf clovers and put them in the basket, just for luck.

When I got home, Aunt Ester peered into the basket over her glasses and frowned. "Why, boy, this all you could find?"

"There's daisies and — "

"Looks to me like you concentrated more on that mustard grass than you did the flowers! Well, I reckon this will have to do. Times a-wasting and no point in quibbling over it. Preacher Dawson will be arriving soon and bringing Fleur with him."

26
Something To Celebrate

"Bib-and-tucker it, boy!" Uncle Clayborn called
out to me from the other side of my bedroom
door. I knew he meant for me to put on my best
store-bought shirt and pants and the new jacket
Aunt Ester bought me just special for Bear's
wedding. A few minutes later, Aunt Ester come
to the door and called out, "Don't forget to spit-
polish them shoes!"

"I won't, Aunt Ester," I called back.

Just as I was pulling on my pants, Bear come
into the room and started gathering up his
clothes, singing and humming and half-laughing
like as if he was some kind of fool.

"I guess you're real happy, ain't you, Bear?"
I said to him, and he answered, "That I am,
son," and went whipping past me with his new
necktie flying and his new wedding suit thrown
over his arm. I reckoned it would be a while
before I saw him again.

When I was dressed I went out into the front

room and looked around. Aunt Ester sure had
fixed things up pretty. The wildflowers I'd
picked was in a big bowl in the center of the
dining table and on each side of the flowers was
some plates and cups for the punch and cake
Aunt Ester had baked. She sure had gone to a
lot of trouble to bake that fine-looking double-
layer cake. Thing was, it looked mighty small
for a wedding cake, but I reckon Aunt Ester
didn't expect no one to show up to help eat it,
anyway.

I walked all round the room listening to Aunt
Ester humming out in the kitchen and Bear and
Uncle Clayborn getting dressed and I felt a deep
sadness for my daddy. Looked like all his friends
had deserted him, and it was, for sure and for
certain, a hard thing to accept. I looked at the
fresh-washed doilies on the tables and the cover
Aunt Ester had thrown over the divan to hide
the holes from Uncle Clayborn's pipe ashes and
the Bible sitting on a table that had belonged to
my grandma, that Aunt Ester wanted preacher
Dawson to use in the marriage ceremony, and I
took in a deep sigh and let it out. It sure was a
lonesome-feeling room for someone's wedding
day.

I reckoned I'd go on down to the barn and
have a look-see on old Miss Pitty-Pat, when I
heard footsteps on the front porch. I hurried to
the winder and peered out, hoping maybe some
of Bear's friends would be there. It was only
Justin, wearing his dark suit and his hair
slicked back.

I went right to the door but when I pulled it

open, I looked to the side of Justin and here come his mama and daddy and Sylvie, all dressed up in a yeller dress with a wide white collar and a bow at the neck and black patent-leather shoes with bows on them, too. She sure was a sight. Mr. and Mrs. Bogart was all dressed up too, and they was both wearing hats, and in Mrs. Bogart's hands was a big dish with a tea towel covering it.

"Good day, Lyon," Mrs. Bogart said with a smile, and Mr. Bogart said, "How you be, Lyon?" and Justin and Sylvie both had big smiles for me.

My heart started to pound with pure gratitude. "Y'all come in," I said over and over like I didn't know no other words.

"Is someone here, Lyon?" Aunt Ester called out as she entered the room.

"It's us, Ester," Mrs. Bogart spoke up and, as Aunt Ester approached, she pushed the covered dish out at her. "This is my best-made blueberry cobbler. You take it and set it out on the table so's folks can enjoy it."

Aunt Ester took the dish and cried, "Oh, glory be! I'm so glad to see you folks!"

Uncle Clayborn appeared and shook Mr. Bogart's hand all the way across the room. Sylvie went off into the kitchen with her mama and Aunt Ester, and me and Justin went out on the porch while Uncle Clayborn and Mr. Bogart sat down to swap tales and have a smoke.

"I bought a doll for Taffy, Lyon. It's got a china head and it cost me all the money I had saved up and all I could borry from my gran'pap.

I'm going to ask Taffy to go steady with me," Justin said.

My mouth went dry. I stared at Justin. If he knew about all of them dolls being broke, he'd probably want to buy her more. "Where'd you find a doll with a china head?" is all I could say.

"A place in Tylersville," Justin answered like he was right pleased and proud of hisself. Then his expression changed. "I reckon you'd ask Taffy to go steady with you, if you was me, wouldn't you?"

My heart was pounding. For the first time since I'd knowed Justin, I wanted to fold up my fist and jab him right in his belly! I wanted to shove him down the porch steps and wrestle him all over the ground, until he told me he wasn't going to give Taffy no old doll with a china head and wasn't going to ask her to go with him. But all I did was nod my head up and down in answer to his question. Looked like Justin was just about as crazy about Taffy as anyone could be except . . . except for me! Well, I was going to leave Clement's Pond anyway, so what did it matter? Like as not, I'd soon forget Miss Taffy Marshall and her dark eyes and that long old braid she was always tossing around.

"Holy jumpin' earwigs! Look yonder, Lyon," Justin said, and I follered the finger he had pointed down the road. "It's old Ferdie and Skeeter and Huey."

I had to smile when I seen old Ferdie. His pants was hitched up to his waist and he had on a jacket with a daisy in the lapel. Both Skeeter and Huey looked like they'd been spit-polished until they shined. When I seen them coming to Bear's wedding, all my bad feelings for Justin disappeared. They come into the yard and Skeeter run up the steps and punched my arm and said, "Hey, Lyon!" and laughed like a little fool.

"Hey, there, Lyon," Ferdie said as he climbed the steps.

I sure was glad to see old Ferdie and them kids. Looked like a few people was going to show up at Bear's wedding after all. Ferdie and Skeeter and Huey went on in the house and I could hear Uncle Clayborn laughing and greeting Ferdie. I reckon he'd gone to pumping Ferdie's hand too.

I'd just turned around from watching Ferdie and the kids go through the front door when I heard preacher Dawson's old Ford clunking down the road. Me and Justin turned and looked as the Ford made its way to the front of the yard and stopped. I could see Fleur's pretty face there sitting next to preacher Dawson. She turned and looked up on the porch and smiled at me and Justin. Preacher Dawson got out of the car wearing his best Sunday preaching coat and went around to open the door for Fleur and help her out. Me and Justin both had to catch hold of our breath as she stepped down from the car.

I ain't never seen ner expect to see no other woman as beautiful as Fleur Portune on that day. She was wearing a white dress that come to her ankles and white shoes and a little satin band around her forehead with a flower in the side of it and her hair was pulled back away from her face and hanging long in the back. She held a little bouquet of flowers in her hand with long streamers of ribbons hanging from it. Me and Justin stared at her all the way across the yard and up to the porch.

"Hello, Lyon," Fleur said after she'd come up the steps.

"Hello, Miss . . . Miss F-Fleur," I stuttered from the pure joy of her beauty.

"Better get in the house now, Miss Fleur, and get you hid before Bear sees you. Bad luck for bride and groom to see each other before the ceremony," preacher Dawson said and he took hold of Fleur's arm and guided her past me and Justin into the house.

I was still reeling in my head from the sight of Fleur when Aunt Ester come to the door and said, "You boys come on in now. It's near about time for the ceremony to start."

"Ester Tarver, don't you let preacher Dawson start that wedding until I get in the house and get to playing the wedding march!"

I looked around and there was Trudence Welch, who played the pianola at the church, hurrying up the steps. She dashed past me and Justin and Aunt Ester, in the doorway, and hurried toward Aunt Ester's pianola.

"Well, glory be!" Aunt Ester said, and I could tell she sure was surprised and happy to see Miss Trudence.

Me and Justin went on in the house and Mr. Bogart called Justin over to him for some reason and right then Sylvie come up to me and said in a soft voice, "I hope you ain't still mad at me, Lyon."

"Naw, I ain't," I said.

"I wish Taffy was here. Just don't seem right for Taffy not to be here," she said, and she looked down at her patent-leather shoes. Her hair looked as white as the collar on her dress and she smelled like the cool, damp grass down by the pond.

"We was bad wrong to accuse Taffy," I said.

"Don't you think I know that?" she said, looking up at me. Then she looked down again and said, "I just wish we could all be like we used to be. Having fun and everything."

"We will be," I said, and Sylvie looked up at me with a hopeful expression on her face. But I started wondering, heavy in my heart, how we could be the way we used to be if I went away. How could it all be the same if, when Bear and Fleur went away, I went with them? A big lump decided to come and pay a visit in my throat.

"Do you reckon your Aunt Ester would mind if I took Taffy a piece of your daddy and Miss Fleur's wedding cake, Lyon?"

I shook my head. I couldn't speak. I was too occupied with thoughts of moving away from Clement's Pond, of leaving my whole life behind me. I thought about my mama's grave up on the hill, and how, if I went away, I might not get to go there for a long, long time.

"I'm going to apologize to Taffy for everything I done to her, Lyon. Oh, I know you don't believe I could ever do that, but I will. You just wait and see," Sylvie went on.

Right then everyone in the house heard a commotion out in the front of the house. Uncle Clayborn and Aunt Ester and the Bogarts went to the door to look see what was going on. Me and Justin and Sylvie follered them and peered out from behind them.

"Look, Lyon!" Sylvie whispered, and her eyes was as big as a sunset.

I looked, all right. Coming up on the porch was Miss Adeline holding Miracle in her arms, and behind her, looked like half the town was clambering across the yard and up on the porch. Aunt Ester swung open the door and Adeline marched in like she was leading a parade, and in come all the rest, big as you please, like as if they wouldn't of missed Bear's wedding for anything in the whole world. The ladies all had dishes of food in their hands and the men couldn't wait to get in the house and go to jawing with Uncle Clayborn and Ferdie and Mr. Bogart.

Uncle Clayborn dashed around getting chairs for people to sit on and pretty soon the whole house was swarming with people I wouldn't of dreamed would come to the wedding after all the mean gossip. But, there they was, all dressed up in their Sunday-go-to-meeting clothes and smiles on their faces like morning sunshine. Even old Ollie Cromwell was there and sneaking out in the backyard every few minutes to do what Uncle Clayborn called "taking a little snort."

I started meandering around the room, my

hands in my pockets, just taking it all in. Everyone I went near was chattering and talking like they'd never had a mean word ner a mean thought in their minds. Looked like Bear's friends hadn't forgot him after all. Looked like, no matter what happened, they was right there just like they used to be. Scattered around the room was Mr. Goad from the store, Uncle Jack, T-Roy Tate and his family, Fulton Kramer and his mama and daddy and sisters and brothers, old man Lyman and his wife, Oscar Bebee, Miss Violet from the millinery shop, and everyone from Sanders' boarding house.

Uncle Clayborn and Aunt Ester come walking by and I heard Uncle Clayborn say, "Look at 'um, Essie. You couldn't hardly say them folks was agin' Fleur now, could you?"

Aunt Ester smiled. "No, Clayborn, a feller couldn't hardly say they was. But I reckon you know it was Adeline who set their minds in the right direction. Adeline and little Miracle."

Trudence Welch commenced to play the pianola and everyone fell quiet. The music filled the whole house with its gentleness and softness. Some of the ladies took out hankies and went to dabbing at their eyes and every now and then someone cleared their throat. And, all at once, I felt like a million butterflies was fluttering around inside my belly. I was that nervous. I slunk over into a corner and set down next to Ollie Cromwell.

Seemed like I was in a daze, because the next thing I knew, Bear and Fleur was standing in front of preacher Dawson and whispers was circling the room and folks was saying things like, "Don't they cut a fine strut together!" and "Ain't that Bear Savage the handsomest thing!" and "I never seen a woman as pretty as Fleur!" "Ohs" and "Ahs" over Fleur's white wedding dress was passed on and sent back again. It was for sure and for certain, Bear and Fleur looked as radiant and fresh as morning sunlight when it first bursts over Clement's Pond and makes everything look like as if it was brand new.

Standing next to Bear was Aunt Ester and Uncle Clayborn and beside Fleur was Adeline holding Miracle. It sure was a sight. Aunt Ester handed preacher Dawson my grandma's Bible and he opened it and his mouth to speak, when Bear spoke up and said, "Just a minute, preacher." And he turned around, looking over the room, up and down, and when he saw me over in the corner with Ollie Cromwell, he motioned for me to come up and stand beside him. When I went up and stood next to him, he winked at me. I winked back. I sure was proud to stand by my daddy on his wedding day.

When preacher Dawson commenced to speak again, you could hear the mice skittering around in the walls, it was that quiet in the front room. Even Miracle was quiet, all big-eyed and listening. Then a sound come that wasn't the mice and everyone turned to look in the direction of the front door. It come slowly open and Taffy stood there in her pretty Sunday dress and them little lace gloves with the holes cut for her fingers and her hair all pulled back and her braid resting on her shoulder and falling halfway down the front of her. My heart didn't beat and my breath wouldn't come. Aunt Ester said time never could really stand still because somewhere, someone was always moving and doing something. But I reckon, for once, Aunt Ester was wrong.

There was a shyness in Taffy's face and it was plain to see she'd been crying. She looked across the room and our eyes met and my heart went to beating again, so loud and so hard it near about knocked me over!

"Come in, child," Mrs. Bogart said quietly to her, and Taffy come into the room and closed the door. "Where is your mama?"

Taffy looked down for a second. Then she raised her head up high and answered, "My mama ain't coming, but she ... ah ... sent her best regards."

Justin moved over close to Taffy and they smiled at each other and went to set down and it struck me what Justin said that time on the bus, about it always being him and Taffy. I reckon there are more than a few things in life a feller has to accept, no matter how it pains him. My eyes run over the room looking for Sylvie. When they found her, she was looking at me. We smiled at each other, then preacher Dawson cleared his throat and I turned to look at him.

"Dear friends, we are gathered together here today to join this man and this woman in holy matrimony," preacher Dawson started, and, next thing I knew, the ceremony was over and Fleur was hugging me and then Bear was near about hugging the breath out of me too.

Old man Lyman had brought his fiddle and he took it up and started playing it and everyone started in clapping their hands in time to the music and slapping Bear on the back and kissing Fleur and wishing them luck and happiness. The ladies started passing out glasses of punch, and me and Justin got into a line that formed around the table where the cake and all the other food set. Aunt Ester and Adeline was handing out pieces of the cake and dishing up cobbler and pie for everyone. Just ahead of us was Ferdie, with Skeeter and Huey hanging at his heels. When he reached out his hand for the next dish of pie, Adeline looked at him like as if she was startled out of her wits.

"Hello, Adeline," Ferdie said with what looked to me like a shy smile.

"H-hello, Ferdie," Adeline said back, and it seemed like their eyes was attached to each other for a long time before old Ferdie finally walked away.

After we got our cake, me and Justin went out on the porch to eat it. Old man Lyman's fiddle was playing a fine soft tune that floated out of the house and swelled over the porch and yard. Every now and then, coming through the music, we could hear folks still congratulating Bear and Fleur and, hearing that and all the happy laughter and chatter, an odd feeling come over me. I started feeling the same way I'd felt when I was looking at my mama's picture, and Justin and Sylvie, and looking at Taffy when she come in the house just before the marriage vows was said. I kept eating the cake and listening to the talk and the laughter and music, and this feeling started growing bigger and bigger inside me. I started shaking my head no ... NO ... NO!

"How come you're shaking your head like that, Lyon?" Justin asked, staring at me.

"What? Oh ... just trying to keep time to the fiddle, I reckon," I answered. But I knew it was because I was studying hard in my mind about leaving Clement's Pond. Fact of the matter, I'd commenced to fight with myself.

Me and Justin left the porch and ambled down toward the barn and Justin said, "What do you want to bet, Taffy and Sylvie foller us?"

I kicked an old tin can that was in my way as hard as I could. It skittered and bounced all the way to the barn, hit the side of it, and come flying back. Then Justin kicked it and it spun back. He kicked it again and said, "Listen! What did I tell you?"

I listened and I could hear Taffy and Sylvie coming up behind us.

I turned and looked back. "Hi, y'all guys," they said, laughing and pushing on each other, and it looked like there never had been a bad word between them.

I started in kicking the can again and Sylvie shouted, "Let me kick it!" and she jumped in front of me and kicked the can up against the barn wall. Then Justin hurried to kick it and Sylvie shoved her foot out, but I got to it first, gave Sylvie a shove, and started to kick it. Then Taffy come up quick and shoved me out of the way and sent the can flying as hard as she could and it hit the barn wall. We all four started shouting and shoving and pushing at each other then, trying to get to the can first. I reckon we played like that for a long time until Aunt Ester called me to come up to the house and tell Bear and Fleur good-bye before they left Aunt Ester's.

As I walked back to the house, I could hear the fiddle music still going strong. I turned once and looked back and Justin and Sylvie and Taffy was still kicking that old can around, jumping and shoving and laughing. I caught sight of Miss Pitty-Pat near the edge of the barn, just standing there staring at them. I looked back at the house, at the old porch that slanted down on one side and at Aunt Ester's washtub that hung near the back door on a nail. I looked all around the yard, the pasture, the fields all yellow now with wheat, and I commenced to run toward the front of the house.

I didn't have to fight with myself no longer. I knew I couldn't leave Clement's Pond! It was the only place I'd ever knowed, the place I'd growed up in, the place where I knowed every clod in the road and every secret back trail and the shriek and call of the wild birds, the look of the meadows in winter, the smell of spring, the way the sun shoots down from the sky in summer, and the way the leaves fluttered in little whirlwinds in all the yards and roads in the fall. It was like as if there was a part of me in all that. And how could I leave Aunt Ester and Uncle Clayborn? And Miss Pitty-Pat and Rhett and Scarlett and . . . and . . . Justin and Sylvie and Taffy?

Bear was waiting on the front porch for me. I went up the steps with the cool, sweet smell of evening rushing all around me. Bear smiled at me and put his arm around my shoulder and started right in to telling me how, after a few days of a honeymoon, him and Fleur was going to have to go over to Tylersville and he didn't know what was going to happen and all. It was then that I cleared my throat real good and moved back to look him square in his eyes.

"Bear . . ." I said, and cleared my throat again. "Bear, I got to tell you this and I hope you are going to understand. You see, Bear, I done changed my mind about leaving Clement's Pond. What I mean is, I been with Aunt Ester and Uncle Clayborn all my life and they maybe wouldn't want me to go yet. I mean, who would take care of the horses and do the chores and . . ."

Bear dropped his arm away from me and looked as deep into my eyes as I was looking into his. "You sure about that, Lyon? You're not just saying these things because you think you wouldn't be welcome, are you?"

I shook my head. "No, sir. I mean what I'm saying."

"Well," Bear said after studying me right smart, "I reckon you got a commitment too, a commitment to all you growed up with."

A few minutes later me and Bear went back into the house and a little while after that he winked at me from across the room to let me know him and Fleur was going to sneak out the back door while everyone was still having a good time. Fact of the matter is, everyone was having such a good time, Bear and Fleur wasn't even missed. Except by me and Aunt Ester and Uncle Clayborn, of course.

"I never would of believed you'd let your daddy go away again without putting up a big fuss, Lyon," Aunt Ester said to me when we was alone out in the kitchen. "Are you growed up on us all of a sudden, boy?"

I smiled and blushed. "I reckon so, Aunt Ester," I told her. "I reckon so."

27
Goodbye, J. Edgar Hoover

After Bear and Fleur's honeymoon they come back just to go again, this time to the judge in Tylersville. Me and Aunt Ester and Uncle Clayborn and Adeline, holding Miracle in her arms, stood on the platform at the train depot waving at Bear and Fleur. We could hardly see their faces through the soot that covered the train winders.

"I wish Bear had let us drive them to Tylersville," Aunt Ester said in a troubled voice.

"Now, Ester, you know Bear couldn't spoon with his new bride iffen we was all jammed into the Chevy with them," Uncle Clayborn said.

"Do you think everything will be all right, Aunt Ester?" I asked.

"Yes, boy. Something tells me it will be. Don't fret now. Things will work out," Aunt Ester answered me.

"They look so perfect together," Adeline said as she lifted Miracle's pudgy little arm and moved it up and down in a waving motion. "Wave good-bye to your mama and new daddy," she said to him, and Miracle made a happy gooing noise and bounced in Adeline's arms and showed his two new teeth.

The train started moving and I remembered the time Bear stood on the caboose and we waved to each other until the train moved on down the tracks and out of sight. A lot sure had happened since that day.

Aunt Ester sniffled and took a handkerchief out of her pocketbook and Uncle Clayborn patted her on her shoulder and said, "Now, Essie, it'll all come out in the wash. Don't it always?"

"Don't you worry, Ester, I have a lot of faith in the order of things," Adeline said softly, and I looked at her face and it shone so bright and happy, it made me catch my breath.

Aunt Ester turned to Adeline and said, "Oh, Addie, you of all people, you out of all of us, ought to be feeling the pangs of loss and . . ."

Adeline held Miracle a little closer and smiled. "Why, Ester Tarver, I'm as happy as if I didn't have better sense! This little feller here will always be partly mine because the Lord first brought him to me. And . . . I'm thinking mighty strong on keeping care of Ferdie's boys. Them two is in such bad need of love. And I've got yards and acres and miles to give to them!"

Suddenly Aunt Ester reached out and pulled Adeline and Miracle both into a big hug. "Oh, Adeline . . ." she said, but then her voice got lost in the sound of the train chugging off down the tracks. I could just see through the sooty winder, as it picked up steam and rushed past, Fleur blowing me a kiss through her fingers.

We stayed standing there until the train and even its sounds was all gone and lost in the day. No one spoke. Even Miracle was quiet. Then Uncle Clayborn cleared his throat and said, "Well, we ain't going to stand here all day, I hope! It's near about suppertime and them horses has to be fed and them stalls cleaned out and . . ." He stopped and yawned and added, "And I'm in sore need of a little nap before the table is set."

Aunt Ester drove us home while Uncle Clayborn rested his head against the door winder and closed his eyes. Me and Adeline and Miracle sat in the back seat and Adeline started singing a pretty song to Miracle that filled up the car like a soft, warming fire. I closed my eyes and started walking down a road in a dream with the song floating all around me.

In the dream, someone was walking quickly toward me. I couldn't make out who it was until he got up on me. Then I saw! It was J. Edgar Hoover hisself! My heart leapt up into my mouth and I started to break into a wild, terrified run, but all that old J. Edgar did was tip his hat at me and walk on by! Even in a dream, I knew it was a good omen.

About the Author

PATRICIA PENDERGRAFT was born in Oklahoma and raised in the central valley of California among people who are very much like Aunt Ester, Lyon and the inhabitants of Clement's Pond. For as long as she can remember she has wanted to write, and she recalls: "As a child, I penned little stories on 'scratch' paper from school, made covers for them and stapled them together. I still have two of those stories written almost forty years ago!" Her intentions of becoming a writer were put on hold while she raised her family, and it has only been recently that she has been able to go back to what she loves most — writing.

Patricia now lives in California and has four children, Tammy, Theresa, Richard and Heidi, and one granddaughter, Lisa Marie.